THE AZURE DREAM

Day of Good News Series

Book 1

J C KLAUDER

The Azure Dream
Day of Good News Series, Book 1
by J C Klauder

Printed in the United States of America.

Edited by Xulon Press.

ISBN 9781545600320

www.xulonpress.com

To my parents,
Dr. John R. and the Rev. Robertha H. Klauder,
whose extraordinary lives
have been grand symphonies;
vibrant, nuanced and compelling.
Thank you for your love
through the varied seasons,
and for the many striking adornments
you wove into the family tapestry.

May the King
who walked lowly among us
greatly bless you.

JC

Table of Contents

DAY ONE

Chapter 1

Into the Arms of Bliss

Stone Lotus Blossom,
Heaven's Lily
white and blue,
teach your secrets
to this simpleton

Reveal,
O, Sweet Sapphire Sea,
and uncover your
azure beating heart to me now

In the folds of your silk robe,
all lapis lazuli,
fringed in turquoise and cyan,
envelop me fully
and swaddle me in the depths,
where your glorious miracle is born,
and the wellspring of wonder overflows

Storehouse,
O, Sparkling Storehouse,
from which the many hues
of sea and sky
across the Universe are loaned

Deep within you lies
the Bluesmith's enchanted forge
and magnificent manufactory,
where underneath, God must sleep,
and there He has
The Azure Dream

Sun Hui Yun could no longer withhold the brush strokes of emotion from painting bold textures across her face. The striking, slender Chinese woman with rather high cheekbones and an ever-so-slightly protruding chin, clothed in the required snow white, thickly-protective body suit and helmet, was as wide-eyed as a child first encountering the magic of fireworks. She pursed her lips and let out a primal sigh of extreme joy and pent-up anticipation. Rocking back and forth and tingling all over, the normally composed Hui Yun was simply overcome, knowing the coveted experience was now so very close at hand.

Was she about to descend "into the arms of bliss" as one rider had recounted? Would "time stand still" as some had observed? Would she find herself or lose herself, or somehow, oddly, both? What concept or illustration could describe what others had categorized, for lack of adequate vocabulary, simply as "the indescribable"?

It was certainly great fortune China's Poet Laureate, Dr. Zhao Zhi, had made pilgrimage to the newly reopened Crater Lake Geopark and apparently solved the dilemma when he put his ponderings to paper. A clear polymer tube descending all the way from the incredibly unique, cone-shaped, evergreen-covered and rock-strewn Wizard Island to the lowest point of the massive lake, six hundred meters below, had been officially dubbed the *Grand Translucent Slide*. However, Zhao Zhi's sublime musings had captured the essence of the adventure so closely, that among the initiated, the *Azure Dream* had become the slide's de facto moniker, with *azuring* the corresponding verb du jour.

At the very bottom of the Dream in an opaque, thickly walled magnifying observation room, surface light from so very far above was, amazingly, visible still. Yet, it was the descent itself that was the real mind-bending wonder. The marvel of peering into the seemingly fathomless expanse of "blue beyond blue" below was only outdone by rolling over on the soft gel cushion and gazing up at the magnificent sky-lit waters overhead.

In the end, however, it was not so much about taking in the observable world of a stunning lake so extraordinarily deep and clear, as it was about something intangible that was the byproduct of it all.

Perhaps this had always been the case. Why, for example, was one driven to climb mountains? Was it truly just to conquer the summits, or was there possibly much more to the quest? An inner yearning one hoped to satisfy, a cognizance or awakening one sought to elicit; were these not the actual goals of the arduous effort? Indeed, most assuredly, they were and forever shall be.

Such peculiarities have always testified to the deep-seated mystery of humanity's interwoven spirit, soul and flesh. The problem in this particular instance, however, stemmed from the natural limitations within mankind itself. For on the Dream the difficulty was never in finding an elusive bliss, as this was available in abundance, but in handling the sheer unmitigated magnitude of it.

Human beings, born to pursue some internal fulfillment, an enlightened epiphany or even a supernatural spiritual encounter, had still never managed anything quite like the Azure Dream before. Apparently, it could push one's "inner processor" towards "a glorious overload of that much sought-after intangible substance."

While on the Slide, a myriad of emotions coursed through the rider's psyche. Obviously, the feelings of awe and wonder were completely overwhelming. Spellbinding, enchanting, mesmerizing; the passenger was simply consumed by a humbling sense of being infinitesimally small, combined with an out-of-body "oneness" with the immense crystal dimension through which they glided.

And, if the experience wasn't fully complete in and of itself, this "deeply spiritual plunge into Mother Nature's womb" (as Zhao Zhi himself had written glowingly), this glimpse into Eternity (as it could, in fact, truly feel) also came with comic relief, those natural born entertainers:

Seals!

CHAPTER 2

Protocols for Initiates

My all-time favorite thought... Surprise!
Zhao Zhi

As Hui Yun bounded further down the hill, a park employee emerged from a one-room wooden building to greet her. She was momentarily startled by his unusual roughhewn countenance; rugged and impressive as the mighty caldera bowl in which he stood. For nearly six decades the punishing high mountain sun and long, harsh winters artfully chiseled Wesley Williamson's distinct features into an uncanny resemblance of the iconic visage on the old Buffalo nickel.

From his earliest days, the Klamath Tribal member quietly tended horses in the lush, spring-fed meadows bordering the Cascade Mountain's endless woodlands. Williamson had emerged from the backcountry of late to take employment at the reinstituted park, in the hope of better understanding what was happening to his world. The Geopark hired him immediately due to his extensive knowledge of the region's flora and fauna, handed down from countless generations. A rather tall and solid man, he wore the standard brown coveralls of a park attendant and kept his long black and silver hair tightly braided.

In a somewhat gentle voice, Williamson explained safety procedures, emergency protocols and sundry other tidbits to be aware of during Hui Yun's descent such as possible nausea, disorientation and a "whole lotta wonder." He put his hand to his neck, indicating for her to tuck in a small flap at the top of her jumpsuit. Then he produced a badge from an upper pocket, verifying he also functioned as a "certified guide" and could show her the greater wilderness region through his special horse-packing expeditions.

"You can call me Wes," he said matter-of-factly.

Sort of ignoring his pitch, Hui Yun instead made inquiry, "I understand the seals of the lake will sometimes accompany a rider."

"Mazamas!" Wes crowed loudly. He immediately spun on his heels to walk the forty paces to the edge of the lake while reciting lines from a memorized speech on general park information. "The Mazama colony of seals, engaging as they may seem, are wild animals and are not to be approached, touched or fed."

Wes produced an old-fashioned key ring from a hip pocket, probably used for various outbuildings. He stopped at a narrow metal pipe protruding a meter high at the water's edge, no doubt left over from older construction, and spoke a two-syllable word she could not decipher. Turning around, he was somewhat animated again.

"There is one very special one," Wes said smiling and then with more deliberate emphasis he called out,

"Bor-is!"

Tilting his head to listen in, he tapped the pipe with the key ring in his hand to the well-known rhythm, *Row, row, row your boat*. This produced a metal-on-metal sound with a slight gonging that resonated inside the hollow cylinder. He continued the cadence, *Gently down the stream*.

Then he walked to the entrance of the Grand Translucent Slide further up the shoreline. Wes now appeared to be talking more to himself, but with the rather over-exaggerated singsong intonation of a hokey sideshow barker.

"The carnival ride... of all carnival rides!"

The Slide was indeed an astonishing feat of art and engineering. The shiny acrylic opening, twice the stature of Wes, was only the tiny "tip of the iceberg." Slidecars were stacked beside a loading area where a mechanical arm was carefully fitting one onto the tracks. Everything was made from clear polymers, so the majestic marvel of Crater Lake would not be diminished in any way. Lovely little sparkling wavelets lapped against the sides all around. Peering into the extraordinary tube, the "tunnel of glass" and the tracks it housed seemed to stretch on forever.

Hui Yun made her way into the sun-bedazzled archway. From the corner of her eye she spotted an anomaly on the pleasant, dancing waves. Soon she could distinguish a dark-furred body, then the nose and forehead of a creature swiftly plying the aquamarine waters along the island's edge. Hui Yun's heart simply skipped with delight!

Boris? she wondered.

CHAPTER 3

The Carnival Ride of Wonder

Vibrations
Splash
Sweet, cool water
Lovely
Glide
Push, glide
Push, glide
Swim happy!
Turn on back
Roll to front
Spot movement
Push hard, follow
Look in eyes
Eyes look back
Good feeling
Very, very good feeling

Boris, a Nerpa seal

Hui Yun lay back trying to relax into her slidecar, but still clung tenaciously to the safety bar.

"When I say so, you will have to let go," Wes remarked.

"Let go?" Hui Yun questioned anxiously.

"Yes," he nodded, indicating the moment was now. She consciously worked to lift each finger from the bar, one digit at a time. She shifted her body from side to side in the cocoon-like stretch netting which loosely secured her to the cushion, hoping to finally settle in. Eventually, both hands were worked free.

"Bon Voyage!" Wes said smiling, as he carefully pressed a floor button with his foot. In a moment the descent began, and Hui Yun was instantly encompassed by the translucent "envelope of splendor" which she had so anticipated. Just as quickly, any of her fears evaporated as well.

Boris made a beeline to the form in the tube and peered in. When their gazes met, she was utterly astonished. How intelligent, how knowing, how warm the seal's countenance appeared. Pudgy and squat, he seemed to have a childlike demeanor; quite happy and playful. He had an ample supply of unusually long whiskers and truly lovely coal dark eyes, so large and engaging, one might even wonder if it were possible to catch a glimpse of the creature's inner soul. Hui Yun was charmed and thoroughly captivated. This was everything she had hoped for and maybe even more.

The crystalline tube was supported by clear columns every four hundred meters and tracked due east past the Lava Dome, across the rocky, gradually sloping floor of the Central Platform. From thirty to one hundred meters beneath the surface, a region of algae growth occurred where occasional wisps of ghostly green clung to the tube. A third of the way into the experience the lake floor further receded, fully engulfing Hui Yun in the numbing blue of the Azure Dream. The Slide then veered south over the Chaski Bay landslide and began a wide circling descent, allowing for observation of the intricacies of the greater bowl on one side and the stellar liquid universe on the other.

Curious, tall silica spires rose in one section of the caldera. In various places, bacterial mats multiplied around hydrothermal vents. Shafts of light pierced the ever mystical and alluring ultra-dark cobalt depths. Yet, most extraordinary of all, was the perspective few had ever contemplated; the view from below the shimmering surface, where the golden mountain sun caressed the great crystal sea. Here, the splendidly sky-infused watery world loomed above, as a dazzling vision of some glorious other-dimension.

Hui Yun became completely transfixed, bathing in the wonderment of it all. Excitement had now given way to a very deep calm. A transcendent peace rolled over her mind. She felt blissful and contented as a baby, happily floating in Mother Nature's womb.

The marvel of this exceptional collection of endless blues almost cancelled out Hui Yun's remembrance of any other color. To the best of her recollection, there was but a lone primary hue in the light spectrum, and she was currently immersed in its grand plunge. It occurred to her this must be the *azuring*, and the term seemed most appropriate indeed.

There appeared to no longer be any reference point to up or down, forward or back, future or past. This was transfiguring to the core of her inner being.

All the while Boris, underwater escort, faithfully accompanied the spellbound rider.

The speed of the Slide was well controlled, so the seal had no difficulty in keeping pace. Occasionally, the animal would grow shy and swim away several meters, then curiosity would get the better of him and he would return to stare into the tube with his remarkable ebony eyes. It was evident that the creature could plunge to tremendous depths as he did not seem at all interested in turning back. Perhaps the fun for Boris was watching the colorful expressions on human faces as they traversed the spectrum from sheer astonishment to being somewhat *non compos mentis* (not in their right mind), as they succumbed to the witchery of the Azure Dream.

Halfway into the descent, while soaking in the breathtaking beauty and splendor of the lake, Hui Yun experienced another curious sensation. A faint whisper became audible in her mind. She shook her head, bewildered. The soft whispering resumed.

It was comparable to some sort of melody.

She studied Boris, who was now swimming very close to the tube, and pondered if, somehow, the mystery had something to do with him.

Hui Yun was suddenly struck with a mind-expanding possibility. *Was there an inner communion occurring with the seal; an actual reading of minds? No, no, this wasn't plausible,* she surmised. Perhaps she was giddy and disoriented from the overwhelming nature of the Slide experience. She looked directly into Boris's eyes and wondered. The animal displayed an expression of quiet fascination, as if he too contemplated the same question. The seal swam off a short distance and began twirling joyfully.

Hui Yun focused once again on the otherworldly realm engulfing her. She was fully overcome. *Had Time itself come to a halt? Had her descent been strangely interrupted?*

Hui Yun was now a billow of wind in an endless clear sky, or was it, in fact, a sea? Yes, an extraordinary sea in which she had always swum, effortlessly, and danced to an ancient haunting melody. Suspended, floating, at peace, she glided toward a curiosity. Peering in, she saw the features of a perfectly serene human face staring back at her. There was a moment of shock, then complete astonishment. A shudder of awe thoroughly shook her from the soles of her feet to the crown of her head.

Boris finally broke off to return to the surface. The stupefied rider continued her descent into the much darker depths, gradually decelerated and eventually entered a space the size of several large living rooms. Hui Yun was now in the observation chamber in the deepest reaches of Crater Lake. Though her slidecar had stopped moving, she was not entirely sure that it had. There was an infinite numbness; mind and body. The blissful traveler could not possibly have known this, but someone was there already and had been patiently awaiting her arrival.

CHAPTER 4

Meet and Greet

At the Wanfu Construction Headquarters,
New Portland, Oregon Territories

Comes forth crimson glow
From the womb of the Dawn,
Day born, day born
As the begotten of man
My spirit, adulation,
Is the dance of the faun
And my glory is mirth,
As the gallop of Pan

Aurora, my queen,
Goddess, my love,
Press to thy bosom
This frailty, my soul
Upon seraph's wings
Would now I, above,
Alight morning star;
Breathe, breathe the celestial

Violent and lovely,
My goddess, my dawn
For shatter the dark,
Though thy weapon be beauty
Wean me not, thy milk sweet
Is the dew thou hast spawned
But alas, thy travail passes,
Day born and thou art gone!
Zhao Zhi

In a nondescript break room engulfed by an enormous, bustling, ultra-modern urban construction project, the lightly framed yet big hearted professor of literature, Dr. Zhao Zhi, addressed his crowd of prospective students and faculty. Though he truly appreciated the great heritage of poetry and prose from the British Isles, he rarely attempted to compose anything in English. Zhi hoped his humble ode in the spirit of the Romantic poets would be adequate for this initial orientation meeting. He had been inspired to write the verse after observing a glorious sunrise while visiting Oregon's high mountain country.

It was a minimal gathering of around forty individuals and Zhi spoke very candidly, almost surprisingly so. Though he was perhaps barely just a diminutive five feet in stature, he commanded a presence that was far larger, thoroughly captivating the room. With kindly smiling eyes behind an old-fashioned pair of wire-rimmed spectacles and a happy round-cheeked face, ever so ready to dole out enthusiastic expressions for others, he exuded a contagious and wonderful charm. The professor had a noticeable Mandarin accent, yet speaking carefully, he could be readily understood. He finished reciting his poem and then looked around the bare-walled room.

"'We know what we are, but know not what we may be'... anyone... anyone?"

"It's from *Hamlet*... I think," one member of the audience said sheepishly, which prompted a little laughter.

"Yes, yes, indeed it is. Now, I do not know who you are young man, but I *do* know what you may be... you... Americans. For you have been an important inspiration to me... my whole life, and even now you remain my reason to press on against this vast sweeping tide. So, may I confide in you all... ah... certain truths you might not wish to hear but, perhaps... should?

"I am aware of particular realities, some good... and some... ah, not so good. I am endeavoring to do what I can to make this transition period for you and your countrymen as smooth and beneficial as possible. The dedication of this small college in New Portland, I believe, is an example of this. Frankly, my government is full of a veritable army of egomaniacal hard-noses, but we have successfully lobbied to maintain English as a primary study here.

"Yes, Chaucer, Shakespeare, Donne, Milton... ah, Swift, Byron, Dickens, Austen... George Eliot, why even your very own Mark Twain, Melville and Steinbeck. No, oh no, your classics should not be forgotten, but preserved and celebrated and... lovingly retold to future and... and all the coming generations. So, today we chart a course for your own... rediscovery... if you will." Zhi stopped and smiled benevolently at the group.

"'It is not down in any map; true places never are.'" He looked about again to see if anyone knew he had just quoted from *Moby Dick*. No, no one apparently had.

Suddenly the professor held out both hands, palms up, and started crooning with unabashed gusto.

"Home… home on the Range. Where the deer and the antelopes pla…ay!"

Those seated in the room exchanged glances. One student mouthed to another, *he's quirky*. Zhi continued exuberantly.

"Oh, ha ha, yes indeed… and the *Great American Songbook*… an important contribution to world literature. Now, where was I?"

"That's from the *Great American Songbook?*" whispered one student incredulous. "I don't know if he's right about that."

Now Zhi grew silent for a moment and stared at the unadorned walls. He continued his very honest heart-to-heart with the small gathering.

"Many things were lost in America after your government fell in 2025. Then, international aid was curtailed after the outbreak of those awful pandemics. For over twenty years, your nation has endured great hardship being placed under international quarantine. But today, here in your lovely Pacific Northwest, we can finally assist in the rebirth of America and her wonderful spirit. I, for one, will not let your own great story die. I have labeled this an era of pageants… and poetry… to celebrate and memorialize your heritage. Yes, pageants and poetry…"

Zhi appeared to be caught away and transfixed on something internal. After a moment, he began an impromptu recitation of Wordsworth's *The Rainbow*.

My heart leaps up when I behold
A rainbow in the sky:
So was it when my life began;
So is it now I am a man;
So be it when I shall grow old,
Or let me die!
The Child is father of the Man;
I could wish my days to be
Bound each to each by natural piety.

Zhi continued mumbling the refrain, "The Child is father of the Man."

Snapping out of his trance, he found himself back in the room, smiled and began singing from his beloved repertoire of American folk music, encouraging the somewhat bewildered group to join him.

Oh, my darling, oh my darling,
Oh, my darling, Clementine!
Thou art lost and gone forever
Dreadful sorry, Clementine…

CHAPTER 5

Encounter in the Deep

Friends are treasure. Great pearls are cultivated as are great relationships.
Zhao Zhi

Hui Yun's slidecar slowly elevated her into a sitting position. She finally shook her head a bit, indicating a partial return to this world.

"Ni hao," came a male voice seemingly out of nowhere.

She turned, dumbstruck, and gazed at a lone man seated on a clear bench in the dimly lit observation chamber. Taking it all in, she began to process where she was.

"Ni hao," she said quietly, still unsure about trying to stand.

"Relax," he said reassuringly, "it's going to take a while."

Hui Yun merely stared, still overcome. Though the light was somewhat weak, she could easily perceive he was a very handsome man. Sporting short cropped black hair, a prominent jaw and wide cheekbones, his overall demeanor exuded a very strong air of confidence. Though he still wore the required white coveralls, it was apparent there was an extremely athletic and muscular individual underneath the thick material. He seemed to be around her age, in his early thirties. She did not recognize him at first, but thought he could be a movie star, or perhaps, should have been.

"I am Qin Jiang," he informed her. "What a delight to meet such a beautiful young woman here on the Azure Dream," he remarked with sincerity and respect.

Normally, she might have blushed, but being a little too delirious she smiled weakly. "I am Sun... Hui... Yun... I think. I'm afraid I must look rather dazed right now."

"It wears off, just take some deep breaths," he said.

After another minute of silence, her voice rang out.

"Qin Jiang!" Apparently regaining some of her wits, she spoke further. "Oh my, how very nice to meet you!"

"No, no, and as the British would say, 'the pleasure is mine, I'm sure,'" he responded.

Hui Yun fell silent again, needing a little more time to compose herself. She was thinking hard. Qin Jiang was well known for something, which was why she had initially become excited, yet now couldn't remember what it was. It should have been obvious, but her mind still wasn't functioning fully. Slowly it came to her. *Of course, you know all about him!*

Qin Jiang was leader of the Feilong 9, an elite military unit made up of notorious, thrill-seeking adrenaline junkies. The severe and adventurous training regimen of the nine "Flying Dragons" garnered endless public attention as they skied the Himalayas, swam cage-free into shark feeding frenzies, dove fearlessly over towering waterfalls, and free-climbed the world's tallest skyscrapers. The group was also known to parachute into typhoons to be wildly tossed by intense winds and then ride out the storm lost at sea with mere float packs, thrashed about by monstrous waves, and consider the whole thing "a splendid outing."

Hui Yun began again with a knowing look. "Well... if you are that Qin Jiang we have all heard so much of, then you would indeed qualify as 'the man' my mother tried to warn me about."

"It sounds like you have regained your composure," Jiang replied. He stood and walked toward Hui Yun, offering her a hand to rise from the slidecar. "It also sounds like you have an intelligent mother," he continued while making a distinct up and down motion with his eyebrows. Then moving his arms in all directions to indicate the opaque glass room of wonder they were both standing in, he declared with emotion, "what a marvelous place to make your acquaintance!"

Feeling much more adventurous than normal, Hui Yun was coy and flirtatious. "I bet you say that to all the girls you meet down here," she said while casting him a look, unsnapping her helmet and revealing her fine, jet black shoulder-length hair.

"Yes, all one of you," he responded with a playfully acquiescing tone and a little shake of his head. Now with her face fully uncovered, Jiang could more accurately study the truly striking and distinctly triangular nature of her facial features; unique and lovely.

Hui Yun then remembered her usual self and felt suddenly shy. It was not unlike Boris the seal, who grew curious, then pulled back and swam away a bit from the rider in the tube. She wondered why she had acted so familiar with a man completely unknown to her.

He broke the silence. "Sun Hui Yun, why you're famous."

"Not at all," she retorted, lips pursed in a disapproving manner. "That was my father." Then she paused a while, looking very intently, straining her eyes at nothing in front of her, but trying to retrieve some distant information tucked away in her brain. Hui Yun was suddenly flooded with images from her past as the pseudo-opiate effects of the Azure Dream wore off.

"I recall your father, Jiang, was an important General."

"I did not want to bring that up here and now, this is not the place or time," he said with some concern, "but, I knew when you told me your name that we had already met."

"Already met? But, I don't recall that."

"We shared the ambulance ride to the hospital…" Jiang trailed off for a moment.

"You were that little boy lying next to me!" Hui Yun said incredulously.

Then he finished his statement, "… after the… bombing."

"I… ah… I remember we held hands on the way."

Neither could speak as they pondered the incident from twenty years earlier, when dissidents attacked a motorcade of government dignitaries and their families. Hui Yun's father had been fatally wounded in the terrifying blast. Now she experienced a powerfully bittersweet moment as she pictured her loving father in her mind, while also reliving the dreadful tragedy once again.

CHAPTER 6

Keep Faith

Hope is the honey of the successful colonies of man. *Zhao Zhi*

"Professor Zhao, we have heard a strange rumor… and so, can you confirm this and explain why there are seals now in Crater Lake?" a student inquired.

"True and… exactly my point, young man… many unusual tales from this long-lost continent," Zhi remarked, while twisting from side to side, looking for any other questions. "And mysteries… ever so many mysteries," he mumbled to himself.

"But you didn't tell us why there are seals," another student called out.

"Well… maybe we should ask them," Zhi replied and everyone chuckled. "Yes, but the greater question really is how… correct? I mean… did they swim straight through the planet all the way from Lake Baikal… immigrating perhaps, those Nerpas? No, no, I don't imagine so. Use your mind, young man. Maybe it was some misguided effort to eliminate all the invasive… nonnative fishes. So, what did they do?

They introduced a far, far larger and intrusive species! Arf, Arf!" The room erupted in laughter.

Zhi had completely won over his audience now. He continued to reveal more information and his overall concerns.

"Oh, this grand dedication they've planned for the Crater Lake preservation… or whatever it is… which I hate to confess I am right in the middle of. It sounds impressive, doesn't it? They have preserved nothing, I should inform you, as your great naturalist Mr. John Muir whirls in his grave. For there are these two gaudy glass hotels and numerous tourists in hover vehicles buzzing every which way over the lake.

"And that endless slide cost billions… yes, billions to build. Such money should have been used to restore more infrastructure in your country. Oh, the contraption is nothing more than a billboard to the world for the massive petrochemical firms. It's a shameless edifice to the hubris of self-absorbed men."

Zhi was momentarily caught away in very deep thought. He looked out the window for a time at the glittering obelisk skyscrapers, interspersed with colored acrylic domes and cubed-shaped buildings. Pointing outside he turned back toward those present.

"And here they're pouring numerous new structures left and right to give you a 'brand new' Portland. Yet, they haven't asked you what you want, have they? I've been told more than half of the city will be populated by those now immigrating. We are not really restoring America. We may, more accurately, be absorbing her. And… there are other things I cannot put my finger on that remain in the shadows. It's just a feeling, but I would have to say that once again, 'Something is rotten in the state of Denmark.'

"Oh, will Mankind ever learn? Every generation imagines it is the enlightened one that will be so very different, yet it never is. Now, take those Romantic poets, will you? Great writers... I admire their work tremendously, and I will never possess such eloquence. Yet, they were dreamers... idealists... prone to living eccentric lives. Not unlike your American counterculture of the 1960s. That was a free-spirited, adventurous time, no doubt... with wonderful, inventive music. But the vision was also wholly impractical, with many fanciful ideals that lead you nowhere, except into insurmountable national debt. Too much of a good thing, perhaps?" Zhi seemed to drift off once again.

"Now, what is it you Americans are calling the new city?"

"Polymeratopia!" a student cried out.

"Oooh, I like that, Polymer... atopia... Ha! No, Utopia it will not be. But, on a brighter note, the clever term shows your poetic spirit is alive and well!" Zhi continued with a happy tone.

"So... you will surely create newly inspired works born from your past struggles... and I imagine... ah... all those to come. 'Poetry is a mirror which makes beautiful that which is distorted.' Did you know that's Shell...?"

"Is there no hope for our future, then?" one concerned student interrupted. The professor turned and smiled kindly at her, trying to be reassuring.

"Hope? Yes, yes, of course there is... there is always hope. Yes... you Americans have buttered your bread with hope for generations!"

CHAPTER 7

A Kitschy Communion

Exposing one's heart is the highest goal of conversation. *Zhao Zhi*

"So you were sent here to research… aah…?"

"Demographics," Hui Yun said plainly.

"Oh, how fascinating," Jiang responded, sounding as interested as he could.

"Qin Jiang… famous global extreme adventurer… is fascinated by my study on demographics? Not even I am so naive to fall for that line."

Unable to hold back a growing smile, he nodded his head. "Okay, you got me, but I'm sure it's important to someone… you know, some old fuddy-duddy in the government bureaucracy." He crossed his eyes and scrunched up a goofy smile, mimicking some fastidious, nerdy character. They both chuckled heartily.

Remembering some manners, Jiang quickly apologized. "I did not mean to belittle your work. No doubt what you are doing is very important as we assess the status of this reemerging America."

"It's technically called Survival Analysis Demography. We want to determine why the Americans who survived… did so. Why did some thrive, while others… could not?"

"Well, you know, that does sound very important." He wasn't pretending this time and thinking about it for a moment, he reflected seriously. "I would imagine it was likely old-fashioned grit and resourcefulness. What is their word for it? Pluck… that's it, and then maybe some good fortune, too. It was pluck and luck, ha!" Jiang was pleased with his rhyme in English and Hui Yun nodded in approval.

I could really start to like this guy, she thought.

The pair entered the exit tube of the Grand Translucent Slide. Here, riders were seated instead of lying prone, and more artificial lighting allowed for detailed observation of the terrain. The acrylic tunnel climbed precipitously up the Merriam Cone, toward the ever-increasing glory of the sky-blue surface and eventually emerged at the well-trodden Cleetwood Cove. It was much shorter than the descent, but no less extraordinary.

After leaving their white coveralls with an attendant, the renewed acquaintances walked toward some floating platforms housing tourist shops. There was a noticeable chill in the air and a good deal of snow still piled in drifts.

"I hope you'll excuse my thrill-seeking nature, but it's very hard to be by water and not desperately want to plunge in… especially, this marvel!" Jiang said enthusiastically.

"What, now?" she gasped. "It has to be near freezing!" The water was, without question, dangerously cold. Frigid enough, she imagined, to cause hypothermia in a short time.

"I won't be long, I promise."

Hui Yun looked on in bewilderment as Jiang walked up to an outcropping perched about five meters over the lake. He removed his shirt, revealing the intricate flying dragon tattoo upon his right shoulder; the telltale insignia of his fabled club. He pulled off his shoes and along with his shirt, tossed them back toward the bottom of the rise. Then, without the slightest hesitation, he leapt out over the water, performing a well-polished, near perfect one-and-a-half with a full twist. If Hui Yun had not been so stunned by all this, she probably would have jokingly said, *Show off!* However, he was not actually seeking attention, he truly could not resist.

Splash! Then Jiang hollered, confirming how brutally cold it was, and swam to a low point to climb out. He immediately hopped into a therma-ring, placed there for just such a purpose. In a few short minutes, the undulating metallic hoops with jets of hot air made him thoroughly warm and dry.

The couple made their way to a lakeside bistro to sit and enjoy a bite of food and more friendly conversation. Hui Yun was surprised to hear Jiang mention how emotional he had become on the Azure Dream. He wished his mother could have lived to see such lovely waters.

Hui Yun wondered if Jiang also felt as if he were in a "womb," but declined to bring that up, nor did she mention the encounter with Boris, which he did not seem to have. She realized that alluding to the episode of "communicating" with the animal would have sounded crazy. Looking out the window, she commented, "when you observe the lake from the shoreline, you have to wonder if they poured in some magical dye, to make it so incredibly blue."

Jiang laughed and nodded in agreement.

Hui Yun now thought about the tranquil world below and for just a moment she was floating peacefully in timeless bliss; gliding, spinning, swimming, playful, joyful, like a seal.

"Are you still with us?" Jiang inquired.

"Oh, of course, of course, I guess my mind is still dazed from the incredible slide... euphoria... ah, please forgive me."

"No need to apologize. I understand completely," Jiang reassured her.

She looked around, studying the somewhat touristy building in which they were seated. The shelves lining the walls were filled with crystalline knickknacks for sale to the newly arriving park-goers. Hui Yun noticed many castle souvenirs and no small number of shiny, smiling seals.

"This is a bit much, isn't it?" she observed quietly, so as not to be offensive.

"Don't the Americans have a word for this sort of thing? Totally... ah... 'tacky,' they call it," he said and they both giggled.

The bistro was associated with the hotel on the eastern rim, the one referred to simply as the "Ice Castle." The structure appeared to be a Disney-esque, fantasy style chateau mock-up, all in acrylics, which might have been perfectly fine for a theme park, but seemed way over the top and certainly out of place at the otherwise unblemished natural wonder of Crater Lake. The dinnerware was the same used at the hotel. Hui Yun had a twelve-centimeter-high replica of the fabled Neuschwanstein Castle rising from the back of her clear plate. Jiang appeared to have the entire fortified City of Carcassonne on his.

Holding up his chopsticks in front of him, Jiang remarked, "and of course, they're clear plastic like everything else."

When the waiter produced desserts on plates containing a reproduction of The Forbidden City, Jiang raised his eyebrows.

"Ha, should have guessed!" Then he observed, "and mochi? That's Japanese."

"Well, so is sushi, we borrowed that also, didn't we?" Hui Yun remarked.

"And, I guess, now we've come to 'borrow' from the Americans." He took a bite of his dessert and exclaimed, "oh, now that's quite good with some real banana! I bet they haven't had any of those in this part of the world in a generation."

"Xiexie," said the waiter, interrupting, as he placed another small plate on the table. This one had a crystal lotus blossom protruding at its back and held, of all things, two classic fortune cookies for the guests.

Jiang rolled his eyes.

"Oh, come now, I've always wanted to try one of these cookies!" Hui Yun asserted. "Now we get to adopt a true Chinese-American tradition. Open it up and let's read our fortunes." Hui Yun pried the treat apart, held up the small paper and read aloud.

"'Divine Love blossoms in the ever-fertile Soils of Surrender.' Hmm, well, that's… interesting, I will have to contemplate that for a while. Read yours, tell me what it says."

Jiang was hesitant as he studied his message for a moment, then spoke dramatically.

"'Silence the Dragon of Late Night Hunger! Bistro on the Cove open daily until 2 AM!'"

"It doesn't say that, you just made it up!"

"Yes, it does, it does, I swear!"

After some elaborate hand-wrestling, Hui Yun did succeed in procuring the fortune cookie paper from him and was amazed to find he had not been fooling. She read it aloud again, still incredulous. Eyeballing one another, they blurted out in unison:

"Totally tacky!"

And they laughed enjoyably for some time after.

Eventually, the pair boarded a shuttle to return to their hotel. The translucent, triangle-shaped vehicle could seat forty-five passengers, but Sun Hui Yun and Qin Jiang were the only riders. The transport driver, in the open cockpit, had enthusiastically waved them in.

Holographic images displayed the unusual park features and Jiang and Hui Yun excitedly identified them together. The unique Pumice Castle, the Phantom Ship, ever embarking on another epic voyage, the Wineglass, partially obscured by snow, the towering Llao Rock and other points of interest in between became the subject of some "oohs" and "aahs."

The driver commented, "she can really work her magic on you."

"What was that?" Hui Yun inquired.

"The lake… I call her 'she'… and when you get the chance, take small transports to investigate her wonders more closely. Oh, and don't miss Llao's Hallway. It's all fascinating… but wait until after the Grand Opening." He pointed at the rim where crews were setting up various pieces of equipment. "Did you mention you just rode the slide? I understood it was closed now with all the preparations going on. Now remember, there are false snow-ledges and dangerous drops, so always keep safely back from the edge."

"Thank you, we certainly will," returned Hui Yun, wondering what he meant by the slide being closed, but did not ask. Instead, she inquired, "and what about the seals?"

"Damn nuisance really, they don't belong here, but folks get too attached, so I don't think we'll get rid of 'em any time soon."

"Where do you find them?"

"Around Wizard Island and Fumerole Bay, that's the spot to look. In a moment, we can see if any are lounging around. In winter, they warm themselves in the sun, but not so much now. The vehicle dipped in on the backside of the island, but the animals were apparently not "at home."

"Oh, too bad," Hui Yun remarked.

The driver explained, "I think the seals are pretty scarce with all the activity in the lake. The other day large teams of men and machines worked underwater, laying out these 'light cannons,' they call 'em."

"Sounds unusual," Hui Yun observed.

"Yeah, they did a test one night. Wow, are you in for a doozy of a show!"

A *doozy?* She giggled at the strange American word.

The transport operator then swiveled his craft around so that Hui Yun and Jiang were facing out toward the lake as they ascended to the rim. The introspective visitors gazed upon the exquisite scene in silence. More than just a mammoth pool of crystal-clear waters, "she" was a universe unto herself, stretching down to unfathomable depths. The twosome perceived they would long remain captive to "her" wiles.

As the craft returned to the Rim Village Airpad, the pair studied the remarkable Diadem Lodge. It was an incredible, ultra-modern array of angular shapes, yet, it was no less out of place than the "Ice Castle." They thanked their impromptu tour guide, then strolled down a path to the edge of the rim to catch one more glimpse of "her" majesty.

Gilded rays of the late afternoon sun appeared to heighten the caldera's extraordinary beauty. A special stillness overtook them as the wind had fully abated. The perfectly calm lake below now became a marvelous mirror, in whose stunning reflection all of Nature's grand handiwork shown detailed and ornate. Not unlike the great Colosseum of old, it was an amphitheater for the ages. They observed the incomparable scene for some time.

"The ultimate blue," Hui Yun finally commented, full of wonder.

"Beyond blue," Jiang countered, and they smiled broadly at one another.

"Today, I feel as though my dreams have come true," she said contentedly.

"Yes, and just imagine what other adventures await us still... in this reemerging world." Jiang now surveyed the horizon and spoke further. "Our official duties won't begin right away, so perhaps we could explore the countryside together." He made it sound exciting.

"Yes," Hui Yun replied, "it would be nice to have an escort. Also, that local man who works here offered to show me the area."

"Of course, the park attendant," Jiang remarked.

Hui Yun looked away at the lake. Having struggled with low self-esteem most of her life, it was a little unnerving to have such a well-known and extremely handsome man give her so much attention.

Jiang moved closer and touched her shoulder. She was affected with an emotional rush but tried to hide it. Thinking intently, he made a profound statement.

"It is curious we should meet here, after all these years. I believe it is no mere coincidence that brings us together." With wide eyes, she stared at him and then still feeling shy, nervously glanced back at the lake. Jiang continued.

"I have a very special acquaintance arriving here tonight that I would enjoy introducing you to. Perhaps he would like to join us on our wanderings, as well. Do you remember the man's name who can show us the area?"

Still in deep thought, she recalled, "it was Wesley. Yes, Wesley Williamson was the name on his tag. I remember because I thought it had a poetic sound to it. But, after today… everything seems poetic."

For a moment, it appeared they might embrace. Hui Yun, her heart fluttering with anticipation, would not have refused a kiss, and under any normal circumstances, neither would Jiang. Here they were, perched on the edge of one of Earth's grandest achievements; Crater Lake at dusk, Creation's crème de la crème, a wild and naturally romantic setting like few others. However, he stepped back and merely posed a question.

"May I call upon you in the morning?"

Hui Yun was flushed, yet still managed a simple nod and then looked away.

The military man walked up the path and when he was out of earshot, spoke into his communicator. "Get me Williamson… 0900. He works here I believe. What? Wes? I guess so… tomorrow 0900. No… no he's not scheduled to… it's you who won't be scheduled, you idiot. Don't you know who I am?"

"Yes, sir," came a reply in his ear. Then he continued walking.

DAY TWO

Chapter 8

Illusions of the Night

My pillow; my magic carpet ride to the complex inner world of Zhi. *Zhao Zhi*

Hui Yun stood on a hillside, stone-faced and unmoving. She wore a white polyester jacket and pants with a matching captain's hat and chin strap. Suddenly, an immense number of dark-haired women in the identical outfit appeared, standing in rows. In the distance, men also emerged; confident, muscular, expressionless, in white uniforms and military hats. It was a vast sea of people that reached to the horizon. The large group took two steps forward in perfect unison.

The sky appeared to darken as clouds formed over the multitude. In another moment, a flock of doves descended and landed on the outstretched arms of the throng in white. Every individual had a bird on their right arm, yet they remained stationary.

Without warning, an overwhelming brightness shone down from the sky. An observer squinted and cringed from the heat. When he could look again, he saw the doves had melted like ice cream into puddles on the ground. The vast array now sported dark black goggles. Far down the line, the company began to march.

It was no longer safe for the onlooker to remain where he was. Moving quickly to one side, he found a path in some dense brush that led down a hill. Yet, in his great haste, he tripped headlong over a root and slipped into a deep, dark hole. The man fell for what seemed quite some time, feeling utterly helpless.

A faint light below became visible and began to grow in intensity. Being stopped quite suddenly, the observer found that he had landed on a gurney in a very modern and clinical-looking room, walled with large, clear panels. It took a moment to focus, but it became apparent that watching him from behind the glass, in numerous rising rows, sat hundreds of the very same army in white, completely still and motionless. A group in lab coats entered with some very odd-looking instruments, greatly unsettling the "patient."

Then Wesley Williamson awoke, breathing heavily. He looked around only to find himself now lying in his own bed in his simple rustic cabin. He lay awake for hours pondering his curious dream. Was he fearing the obvious; what could inevitably become an overwhelming migration? Or, was it something more troubling altogether, the still somewhat unclear intentions of the newcomers?

CHAPTER 9

Adventures, Adventures!

Though important, the ordinary days pass quietly into the shadows. It is our journeys of discovery which loom large in memory. So, fly little birdie, launch forth and fly! *Zhao Zhi*

Hui Yun awakened to the delightful, high mountain sunshine pouring into her room; golden, liquid, and radiating life. The splendid view from her window was a cloudless blue horizon atop those precipitous caldera walls with the great sapphire lake shimmering far below.

Last night she had tossed about until the sensation of floating had returned. There was a session of dreams, but only one stood out in which she repeatedly looked in a mirror, only to find her reflection was actually observing her.

Jiang messaged Hui Yun inviting her to join him on an exploratory outing after breakfast. He gave instructions to wear layers for any changes in weather, and that she was to meet a renowned VIP, whom he still would not name. *Oh, how cruel of Jiang to make her wait like this*. Yet, she was very pleased to be able to see him again.

Hui Yun hurried to wash, dress and prepare for the day. She was indeed "little girl excited!"

After a quick bite from the restaurant buffet, she walked briskly toward the airpad a mere two hundred meters away. In the distance, she saw three men conversing on the main landing pad. One was small in stature and perhaps elderly, the other two were, of course, the handsome Qin Jiang and the tall local guide, Wes.

The unknown man wore a tan cloth bucket hat that seniors wear on such occasions, matching tan trousers, a red and black plaid shirt and some ancient looking, but rather well-preserved, canvas sneakers.

When Hui Yun was a short distance from the group, Jiang cast his attention toward her and the other individual turned in her direction. Hui Yun stopped immediately in her tracks. She instantly recognized the very famous visage now gazing at her, smiling; one that any and every citizen of the People's Republic could sketch from memory, they knew it so well.

He was, in essence, the very image of China itself. Undeniably a little man, but clearly large of heart, he walked toward the now frozen Hui Yun with a childlike exuberance that was most reassuring. Qin Jiang joined him and after a few paces called out.

"Sun Hui Yun, meet Dr. Zhao Zhi."

Zhi bowed respectfully, but Hui Yun just stared. The notable visitor then struck a small pose and recited in a somewhat feeble attempt at an old British accent, "'Was this the face that launched a thousand ships and burnt the...'"

Jiang coughed and interrupted, apparently thinking Hui Yun would become embarrassed by Zhi's grandiose manner.

The kindly old gentleman then continued in Mandarin. "It is truly a pleasure to meet you, Miss Sun. I spoke with your father once... a true visionary." She remained quiet.

Jiang resumed with his own flowery show. "The distinguished Dr. Zhao Zhi said he would be delighted to join us in touring the countryside. So, we get to enjoy the company of our country's elder statesman. One who in all things shows us what it means to be ever so truly Chinese."

"Enough!" Zhi protested, shooting a glance at Jiang. "I am merely a professor, nothing more... nothing less. So, let us begin our expedition, for it is a matchless day to explore a new world."

Jiang motioned to one side of the airpad where three miniature crafts had been set aside for the travelers. Two of these, with open-cabins, were MACs (Mobile Aerobotic Cubicles) and universally referred to as "mackies." This type of hover vehicle could hold up to two people standing upright, but not much else. The other flyer, a sit-down model with a full enclosure, triangular wings and a tri-blade landing support, was called a Pteranodon. This was, no doubt, for the elderly Zhi to ride in more comfortably. These small personal transports, generically known as "hummingbirds" due to the high-pitched buzz of the air jets, were entirely made of clear acrylics.

The group took the short walk to the units. Prepared safety packs lay beside each vehicle, and the excited explorers set about putting them on. Jiang playfully tugged on Hui Yun's belt strap to test the tautness, and then jovially spoke to her.

"Ready to go adventuring, Miss Copilot?"

Hui Yun feigned a serious look and comically replied, "aye, aye, Captain!" Then she even gave him a quick salute. They both laughed and stepped aboard smiling.

Zhi seemed to be taking some time getting settled into his vehicle. Jiang spoke loudly in an attempt to be helpful.

"You press the button atop your toggle."

"Mahler!" came the elder statesman's reply, as the sound of brass and strings were heard emanating from within.

"Oh my," sighed Jiang, as he dismounted his mackie to walk over to Zhi's transport. The professor raised the visor top and the vibrant music spilled out freely.

Beaming euphorically, Zhi looked at the commander and said, "I will be indulging in Mahler all day!" Then the enclosure was lowered once again.

"Listen, you press the button..."

"I think I know how it works." Zhi's confident voice was now muffled.

Jiang tried again, this time louder. "You press the button atop your toggle, but don't have your foot all the way down on the pedal."

"I know how it..."

Whoosh!

At that instant, Zhi shot straight up like a rocket about half a kilometer in just a few seconds.

Jiang winced. "That certainly has to hurt! The distinguished Dr. Zhao Zhi just left his poor little stomach down here on planet Earth!" The commander turned his head slightly to the left to speak into his communicator.

"You okay?"

After a moment, a rather feeble response was heard.

"Ah... ah, yes... ah, no... I... really don't know... for sure."

"Let's go," Jiang remarked, addressing the other two. "The old man may not even make it through the day. And then what? All of China will never forgive me. Can't have that... now can we?" He shook his head with a little humorous reflection on the moment.

Jiang and Wes both started their transports.

"Hold on tight," the military man reminded his female passenger.

Swoosh, whoosh! In a flash, the mackies ascended to join Zhi's craft. The view was tremendous in all directions, with seemingly endless visibility in the clean mountain air. Hui Yun gazed upon the magnificent wonder glistening below.

Magic, pure magic, she mused.

CHAPTER 10

Mother Nature's Allure

Majestic Dance
Birds of wonder
Water walkers

Let us imagine
You and I are grebes
O how our supple necks twist and bend

And you my friend
Will you dance the wondrous dance with me,
Race atop the waves
Defy all gravity, protocol, impossibility?

I cannot race alone
I dare not
But together, could not we
Some marvelous legend-makers be?

Let us lift one another high
The Dream, even the sky,
Will be ours

Majestic Dancers
Birds of wonder
Common birds
Who, inspired together,
Simply walk atop the waters
Zhao Zhi

Wes led his traveling party down the slopes of old Mt. Mazama over the forested wilderness. Soon a deep ravine opened, and Wes guided the hover vehicles to further explore it. The group observed some fantastically narrow earthen spires which had eroded from the shear canyon walls.

"The Pinnacles," the tour leader informed, as he pointed at the unique features. They all took a few minutes to study the curious formations and then Wes continued on to the large sun-drenched valley in the distance. Here, he directed their attention to many clear flowing springs which disgorged entire rivers from the subterranean world, bountifully supplied by an immense aquifer.

Disembarking and walking toward the birth place of the Wood River, Jiang marveled at the translucent pool which simply appeared out of nowhere amongst the evergreens. He seemed to be studying the area very carefully. "A fabulous source of fresh water," he stated nodding his head approvingly. After another minute of taking in the scene, he inquired of Wes, "and what of wildlife?"

"My stables are not far. We can explore the wilderness quietly, so as not to disturb nature."

The military commander was most annoyed. "I told you already we're not riding horses through the woods. We are not cowboys! We'll fly in the transports."

"These were not meant to leave the park… limited range and all," Wes tried to explain.

"Nonsense," was all Jiang said and then a moment later he repeated, "and the wildlife?"

The genteel park attendant acquiesced and headed back toward the vehicles. They rose above the trees to behold the broad valley and its large lake stretching to the south. A commanding, high, white volcano was far in the distance. The wilderness expert scouted the forest-covered foothills, looking for meadows and clearings and slowed down when he spotted what he was after.

The others flew closer to investigate and hovered with him above a large herd of the rather elegant and horse-sized member of the deer family; the North American Elk. The animals were aware of the intruders but did not flee, perhaps also being confused by the airborne observers. The regal adults grazed and relaxed, while the spring calves nursed or skipped happily about. The explorers lingered a while, enjoying the pleasing scene.

Next, Wes directed his transport over a marshy area with some tall reeds and a myriad of narrow waterways. He searched the channels below until he found the activity he was looking for. The group caught up as Wes paused mid-air. Beneath them, rolling and frolicking in the water, was another wonder to behold; a family of river otters at play. Hui Yun gasped with delight and Zhi clapped his approval. The next few minutes were spent happily watching the tireless antics of the lovely creatures. Hui Yun even mused *these playful otters are like Boris, in miniature!*

Jiang called to Wes, "what is at the other end of this lake, more wildlife?"

"Yes, but twenty miles from here… too far for these vehicles, maybe."

"I'll take responsibility." Jiang was firm.

The tour continued south over the unusual meeting place of distinctly different waters; one blue and refreshing, the other green and swamp-like. They flew over two large, hilly islands and scanned the varied terrain around the now increasingly narrow lake.

As they approached the southern shore, Wes spotted a group of a dozen pelicans on the horizon. He pointed and led the group to the giant birds. The travelers fanned out somewhat, with each wanting to get as good a view as possible. Wes was just behind the farthest bird on the left. Jiang and Hui Yun were above on the right, looking across the ballet of wings.

Zhi put his craft just a few meters directly underneath and laid back so that his hat fell off, revealing his mostly balding head. He was wide-eyed and smiling. Even with the whirring buzz of the hummingbirds, Zhi's bubbling happy, "Woo-eeeeeeee!" was loud and clear on the group-link communicator. The rest were all giddy and filled with enthusiasm too, with the wind in their faces on this gorgeous, sun-filled, cloudless day. It was a pristine moment. This new world they had come to was simply full of surprises and wonders. The joy of the band of adventurers was truly palpable.

Hui Yun pondered, *pelicans are somewhat underappreciated*. She had always seen them as comical and homely, but now realized how wrong she had been. These were astonishing birds, stunning to behold high in the air. They reminded her of antique jumbo airliners. Yes, the beak was ridiculously large, but it was a tool that could be wielded with uncommon dexterity. Pelicans were certainly unique and fascinating, after all.

The presence of the onlookers finally alarmed the large-winged creatures enough that the avian contingency broke apart. Wes flew out in front to indicate it was time to continue to their destination. He changed direction back toward the southern shoreline and signaled they would be landing there.

As Jiang and Hui Yun's mackie descended below thirty meters, there was a sudden sputtering in its power-jets. The craft lurched forward, and though she grasped a handle hold tightly, for a terrifying split second, Hui Yun was sure the momentum would send her tumbling into the air. This was the one danger zone for these devices. At this height, a safety pack might not open in time to do much good. However, Jiang seemed to correct the problem quickly enough to avert a disaster. They touched down unharmed with no further incident. Jiang stormed off the transport furious, swearing at Wes and the unreliable vehicle.

The visiting party found themselves in a very different place than the truly alpine climes of the Geopark. Here, cottonwoods, oaks and willows covered the area, with the pines and evergreens further back on the hillsides. The lake water was turbid; a very distinct and brackish green.

"Well, this isn't as impressive as all that crystal-clear water we have been seeing," Jiang spoke up, still fuming, but perhaps spoke accurately for all the foreigners.

"Oh, now you'll have to trust me," Wes declared. "This region has a beauty all its own. Don't they have a saying in your country such as 'don't judge a book by its cover?'"

"Of course, we do," intoned Jiang. "Confucius said something to that effect, right Zhi?"

Then, striking a pose as if he were on stage, Zhi clasped his hands at his midsection. He turned his head in a comically overdramatic fashion, and with deliberate hokey intonation, articulated slowly.

"Con… fucius say… 'No matter where thou goest… well… there thou art.'"

Hui Yun grinned and laughed heartily, realizing Zhi was making a wonderful funny. He was indeed a delightful little man. Jiang did not seem to find it amusing and scrunched up his face, offering a disgusted little rant.

"What the heck is that supposed to mean?"

"No, listen," interjected Wes, "these waters are dark and murky because they are full of life! It's the clear waters that don't actually have as much living in them. Look around you."

Taking in the surroundings, they noticed he was not incorrect. Red-winged blackbirds and a striking yellow-headed one danced about. There were cormorants and a great variety of ducks. Gulls and swallows were flitting every which way. A regal pair of Canada geese made a showing with their fuzzy yellow chicks in tow. Great blue herons and white egrets stood still as statues in the shallows, while a symphony of songbirds filled the air.

Wes continued. "You never see large flocks on Crater Lake, but here birds by the thousands pass through migrating, for there is abundant food. This time of year, we have pelicans as you enjoyed, but right now the most favored guest is this fellow." He drew their gaze to a group of somewhat slender birds that dotted the water here and there, white-throated with a black-crested head and back.

"We have grebes in China," stated Jiang somewhat uninterested, "common birds."

"Not like these," Wes declared as he waved his arms, encouraging them to pay close attention.

The grebes, often in pairs, dove under the brackish water to forage. They made many curious movements with their remarkably flexible necks, mimicking each other. Wes explained this was part of their courtship ritual. After studying the creatures for some minutes, the guide produced a pocket visualizer and proceeded to manipulate its settings. The visitors could see he was new to the technology but did not attempt to interrupt him.

Eventually, he brought into focus a grebe couple heavily enraptured in its head-twisting Tango. The birds now loomed two meters in height on the emitted airscreen. When they paused for a brief instant face to face, Wes cried out,

"Watch this!"

Suddenly, the grebes rose above the water in perfect unison, and began racing across the surface with a dizzying fast-footed motion and a very distinct cobra-like head and neck posture. The stunning birds covered about seven or eight meters before making a deliberate beak-first dive under the green. It was extraordinary and completely unexpected.

The travelers were spellbound and open-mouthed, letting out a number of "oohs" and "aahs."

"Incredible! You didn't tell us about that, Wes. Oh, I hope they walk on water again!" Hui Yun exclaimed.

The guide was quite pleased with himself, but still spoke very casually. "Every so often, the bird couples do their "rushing" dance… during this season."

I will write a poem about this… one day, Zhi mused, nodding his head with approval.

CHAPTER 11

Unexpected Intersections

My second all-time favorite thought...
I am not alone! *Zhao Zhi*

As Hui Yun pressed a straw into a box drink, Zhi took note and waxed lyrical once again.

"Quaffing, as your taintless way is, from a chalice, Lucent-weeping out of the dayspring."

Jiang made a face. Pretending to be ashamed, Zhi looked down and mumbled softly,

"Francis Thompson."

Wagner's *Ride of the Valkyries* suddenly resounded, and the elder statesman moved off, mentioning he must take the page. A holographic image of a man at a desk appeared in front of Zhi, who could be heard in the distance arguing. The professor returned to the group, red in the face.

"Oooh!" Zhi intoned rather animated. All eyes were on him, so he continued. "I have just met with the new college... a wonderful group. But it appears no funding can be approved to hire local faculty. No, we must assign loyal members from our… beloved Party, no doubt. Oh, how I tire of meddling… fastidious… bureaucracy."

No one spoke. He lamented further.

"Why must every endeavor for what is valid, be the uphill kind?"

Turning slowly around and stepping toward the lake, Zhi quoted from *Macbeth* a verse he knew only too well.

"They have tied me to a stake; I cannot fly,

But, bear-like, I must fight the course."

The ensemble spent a relaxed hour on the lakeshore eating a simple lunch of pressed meal bars and fruit juice. The group observed a few more enjoyable "rushing" displays from the grebes, and other sights and sounds of the rather vibrant environment. Growing a bit more accustomed to their surroundings, the explorers began moving about when Hui Yun spotted a new curiosity.

With their eye-catching and peculiar staccato bobbing motion, quail wandered deeper in the forest. Hui Yun approached closer and was startled to find dozens of the interesting small birds with ornate head feathers in the underbrush. They did not fly away, but scurried on foot, so she followed them.

Wes took note and quickly stood. "Ma'am, I do not believe it is a good idea to venture further up the hillside." Jiang and Wes exchanged looks. Realizing there was something of concern to their guide, Jiang leapt up to accompany her.

Hui Yun had not heard the precaution and kept briskly moving into the very dense growth, hoping to observe more of those strange birds. The military man took almost two minutes to locate her, and when he did it was because she had stopped completely still. Jiang looked intently where Hui Yun was gazing. There, partially visible amidst bushes and tufts of high grass, was a low stone wall, perhaps less than a meter high.

This should not have been surprising or even that interesting, as the entire nation was now littered with the debris of former habitations, with the ruins of its vast infrastructure. Yet, Hui Yun was so newly arrived from China that her first actual glimpse of something, even as inconsequential as this small rock wall, apparently brought home the reality of the fall of the once renowned United States.

What will she say when she sees the burned-out hull of an American megacity? Jiang contemplated.

Hui Yun moved her head slowly, studying the area closely. She made her way about five meters to her right and stopped again. Jiang came to her and looked. In the groundcover, a relatively well-worn footpath was clearly evident.

Others have been here too! they suspected.

Without speaking, Hui Yun and Jiang crossed the wall and cautiously continued. They both surmised the area had been a public park in earlier times. Suddenly, there was the snap of a twig and a great commotion with the whirring of numerous wings, as the meandering quail took flight. There was more movement in the underbrush. *A startled animal, perhaps?* The investigators could not tell.

Walking around the thicket, it was Jiang who stopped abruptly in his tracks this time. Hui Yun came to his side but could not spot anything unusual. He motioned with his head for her to look slightly to her right. She stood amazed as she distinguished a pair of wondering eyes staring back at her from the cover of a bush.

Perhaps no more than four, a precious little girl lay hiding, quiet and still. Her face spoke volumes. It somehow seemed both inquisitive yet knowing at the same time.

"Hello, young lady… and how are you today?" Hui Yun said in her best possible English as she descended to one knee.

After a long silence, the child, bolder than one might expect under such circumstances, crawled out of her leafy enclosure, stood up and approached Hui Yun. The youngster wore a vibrant lavender tie-dyed sun dress and ornately beaded leather moccasins. She had lovely, long, thick, wavy brown hair, which was slightly tangled, but it was her sparkling emerald green eyes which immediately enthralled the visitors.

"Are you an angel?' the darling child inquired.

"What?" Hui Yun asked with the small laugh that accompanies astonishment. "What is that, sweet one?"

"I saw you come from the sky and you are so beautiful. That is how angels are."

Jiang now raised his head, observing that in the vast undergrowth around them, dozens of children and adults had been crouching. One by one they began to emerge, mostly clothed in apparel made from leather hides. Many of the youth wore long hair with interwoven feathers and shiny trinkets.

An older, weatherworn woman draped in layers of skins and aging fabrics moved toward Hui Yun and the girl.

"Come to Nanaw, Little Gracie, come with Nanaw now." She held forth a wizened hand, entreating the young child to take hold.

"Wait," called Hui Yun, "who are you?"

"Well," Nanaw responded while casting a piercing look at the newcomer. Then, turning her head from side to side to indicate the others, the woman tightly closed her eyes and declared emphatically,

"We are… *America*."

Hui Yun felt an enormous charge of emotion emanating from the final word.

After a few moments, Nanaw opened her eyes, redirected her intense gaze at Hui Yun and retorted, "the real question is, who are y'all? And just what are *you* doing here, exactly?"

"We are here to help you," Hui Yun stated kindly and would have continued, but was interrupted by a terse inquiry.

"Didja bring medicine?"

"Well, not today," Hui Yun was trying to be polite, "but we will return."

"We sure coulda used some a few years back. Sickness came through and took botha Little Gracie's parents."

The grandmother grabbed the small child's arm and retreated towards the entangled grove. Gracie, however, did not remove her eyes from the pretty Chinese woman and the girl kept her head turned around as she was walked away. Hui Yun opened her mouth to speak yet could not think of anything to say.

Jiang, furious Wes had not told him of the presence of the villagers there, stepped away from this encounter to confront him. The guide reminded Jiang that the request had been to see water sources and animal life, which was exactly what they had been shown. Jiang stormed off angrily, knowing this was, in fact, correct.

A few minutes later, the military commander made his way back to Hui Yun. He spoke calmly, but quite firmly to her.

"You cannot promise these people all types of aid. We are on information-gathering assignments, not some sort of mercy mission."

"I just thought we could encourage them somewhat," she responded.

"Their lives will improve, but not overnight. It is true, we have come to interact with these people and now is as good a time as any." Looking around, Jiang called out, "aah... Wes, introduce us to the timid forest people, will you?"

"Yes, higher up the hill," Wes informed as he began cutting through the wild bushes.

The village meeting place was a clearing beneath stately, red-barked ponderosa pines. Concrete picnic tables scattered about bore witness to the former park, and thatched huts and lean-tos in the surrounding forest confirmed its current function. Wes explained this was a seasonal dwelling place and that these folks wintered in a lower valley over the mountains. What drew them here from spring to fall was the plentiful abundance of the area.

The local inhabitants began to assemble. There were perhaps upward of three hundred individuals, many of whom were children. No one spoke, they merely stood silent and still, as the villagers and newcomers studied one another. Hui Yun could see the "survivors" represented a mixture of races. Their distinct cultural attire included striking hand-tooled vests, pants and skirts made from colored leather and fur. The youth sported elaborate earrings and ornaments worn in their long flowing hair, made from what appeared to be old-style computer circuitry.

Jiang motioned to their guide to say something.

Wes hesitated, recalling earlier days spent teaching these very people essential survival skills. The tribal member had demonstrated native hunting and trapping, the tanning of hides, his unusual lake-skimming arrows used on resting waterfowl, and the weaving of Tule reeds to create floor mats, screens, baskets and even canoes. He had instructed them on the uses of the numerous edible and medicinal plants of the entire region; chokecherries, huckleberries, wild celery and plum, the abundant sagebrush and the important, tasty staple which dwellers of the marshlands had prized for millennium, the lovely wocus water lily.

Though Wes had assisted these villagers before, he suddenly felt at a loss on how to address them now, especially in light of his vivid nightmare. If it had any meaning, it was his fear that increasing waves of the outsiders could take control by sheer numbers alone. He just mumbled a little until he was interrupted.

An elderly voice spoke out, deliberate and clear. The community gave its attention to the unassuming, small figure.

"I am Zhao Zhi and I have come from far away, from the People's Republic of China, as you may have guessed. I am an old man now who has seen… as you… and I think you will know the reference… 'the best of times and the worst of times.'

"When I was young, I believed in a magnificent dream, as did many others. One day, we gathered at the great square of our capital and raised a statue not unlike your own… Miss Liberty. We rallied for freedom… democracy… significant ideals that had made your country a light to the world." Zhi, now reliving momentous events and still agitated from his earlier confrontation, was suddenly overcome, but labored to continue.

"My wish is to help you rediscover who you... as Americans... truly are. Yet... I am afraid also... for our peaceful demonstration was overrun. Friends of mine disappeared... and were never heard from again..." Zhi dropped his head.

Hui Yun, thinking this had become a bit odd, stepped forward to help and declared, "I am Sun Hui Yun, this is Zhao Zhi, Qin Jiang and Wes, I believe you know. We are very pleased to meet you."

"I am Ted Norquist, Mayor of Pelican Cove," said a balding man from across the clearing, "you are most welcome here. We have long known this day would come... and so we have prepared. Please allow us to give you a proper greeting."

A bushy haired man stepped forward, faced the assembly, raised his hands and mouthed *one, two, three*.

Suddenly, pleasant singing began, and the Chinese guests were immediately impressed. The choral piece conveyed a childlike awe of God and the wonders of His creation. Little Gracie had a solo which she sang forcefully. Her counterpart, a freckle-faced three-and-a-half-year-old boy in lederhosen, could not hit the notes or pronounce all the words, but everyone smiled at his adorable effort.

Who am I, who am I, who am I... I... I? (Girls)
Marvels in the sky at night,
Moon and stars that shine so bright,
Your finger-work is a delight,
O Lord, our Lord, majestic (Girl Soloist)

Who am I, who am I, who am I… I… I? (Boys)
Joyful thinging do we bring,
Honoring our mighty King,
In all the earth let praithez ring,
O Lord, our Lord, majethic (Boy Soloist)

What is man that you take thought of him?
What is man? (Men)
Who are we to reign over the earth
with authority? (Women)

The Heavens offer glimpses of
Your glory and your worth,
O-O-O Lord, our God,
O-O-O God, our King,
Your Majesty, what majesty displays in
all the Earth (Ensemble)

When the performance concluded, the guests cheered enthusiastically. The mayor made his way to the visitors and offered them seating on split log benches at the edge of the clearing.

"Simply wonderful!" Hui Yun cried.

"Well, thank you very much, Sun Hui Yun." Ted took pains to pronounce the name correctly. He then shared, what was apparently, a local adage.

"Minus machinery, admire the scenery."

Hui Yun and Zhi nodded with approval as Ted continued.

"It's a phrase about appreciation… I would imagine. You know… we simply had nowhere to go at night… not even a fast food joint!" The guests smiled at his obvious little joke. "But, as a community we ultimately learned there was power… a power in song… to build up our hope, to strengthen our kinship... and most important, to honor and seek His favor," he said pointing to the sky. "As it is written, 'God opposes the proud, but gives grace to the humble.'"

"Is everyone in your country so religious?" quipped Jiang.

"Don't know about the rest of America... hoped you might be able to inform me. But, in our little village, yes... indeed, we are." Ted shifted on his seat and began anew. "You know, it's actually the children who have inspired us. The young'uns seem to have remarkably keen spiritual senses. They often dream of extraordinary things and occasionally see angels among us. And... they too simply love nothing more than to sit under the stars at night and sing."

"'And a little child shall lead them,'" injected Zhi, pleased with himself for recalling an appropriate quote from the Bible. The mayor smiled at the phrase and then finished his thoughts.

"Yes, many of us have carried a great burden since the *Humbling*." (This was the first time the guests heard the use of this term, but before their stay was over, it would be referenced dozens of times.) "However, the children never knew the world we lost, so for them life does not seem overly harsh. Indeed, this new generation has been a most unexpected surprise in our otherwise greatly diminished existence." Everyone appeared to think on this information for a minute. Then Hui Yun made an inquiry.

"Why, at first, did you hide from us?"

"We were simply observing, not actually hiding. We've all just been watching and waiting," Ted informed her.

"Waiting for what?"

"The next phase, I imagine."

Hui Yun looked at him somewhat perplexed. He explained further.

"A few years back, one of your naval vessels sailed into a large coastal bay. The locals were thrilled and came running to the piers. It was the first contact in over twenty years! One overly eager old timer ran to the long-awaited visitors, crying out, 'Konnichiwa! Konnichiwa!'"

Hui Yun gulped, knowing the mistake of using a greeting in the wrong language might be considered insulting.

"One of the sailors put a knife to the old man's throat, but the captain stopped him from doing any harm. He simply spat on the ground and said, 'No konnichiwa.' Then they boarded the ship and sailed away."

"Oh my!" she exclaimed.

"So... word quickly spread that these outsiders were not here to bring assistance, but were just merely scouting," Ted explained.

Hui Yun's heart burned within her. *I am here to bring aid,* she said to herself.

"When the crews arrived at Crater Lake, we merely watched from a distance... and waited." Now the mayor fell silent.

A small number of adults had gathered around the visitors to learn what they could. Noticing the group and feeling newly inspired, Zhi stepped forward to address them.

"You know, my ancestors wore a queue... a long ponytail... for centuries... then abandoned the practice. Now, it is only a distant memory. My grandmother experienced foot binding as a small girl, but was spared when the missionary, Gladys Aylward, helped end this in her village. Later, my grandmother successfully fled to safety from a terrifying invasion... on foot!

"You see changes come... and go... governments come and go... yet the human spirit endures."

Zhi looked at the carefree youth running and playing around them. The children's joy was infectious. Glimmering sunshine reflected off the jewelry in their free-flowing hair. The atmosphere was idyllic. The professor smiled encouragingly and then concluded his soliloquy.

"Yes, changes will come. But consider your astonishing little ones, are they not promise enough? No matter what befalls you... you have a very bright future, indeed."

"Oh, Zhi!" voiced Hui Yun with emotion, quite affected by his words.

Then a commotion began at the far end of the gathering place and many of the villagers moved in that direction. Hui Yun saw horses laden with bundles coming into view. The procession made its way to the clearing and everyone pressed in like eager children to observe. The horses were draped with a variety of game; deer, antelope, jackrabbits, colorful pheasants, ducks and geese. A dozen hirsute men in well-worn buckskins also arrived, evidently the corresponding hunting party.

A team of residents wasted little time in retrieving the provisions from off the fine Appaloosas. The scruffy woodsmen appeared to be fit men in their twenties and thirties, but two or three were wiry, with very youthful-looking faces, so Hui Yun surmised these were likely only in their teens. Now, bringing up the rear of the hunting party, a horse-drawn cart came slowly over the hilltop.

"You will want to see this!" Ted announced as he led the visitors a short way up the path to meet it. When the guests peered over the tall-sided wagon they simply stared in amazement. There, laying neatly butchered, were the limbs of an immense animal, elephant-like in appearance, but unknown to them.

"Chimera!" Zhi and Jiang finally cried out in astonishment.

"Mammoth or mastodon, we're not sure, exactly," explained Ted. "We first spotted one five years ago and then the beasts moved into the marshy region to our south."

The newcomers studied the curiosity for a while, then walked back to the central gathering place. As they did, they watched one of the teenage hunters throw an object with great precision into a group twenty meters away. The projectile, a small pinecone, found its mark as intended between the shoulder blades of another teen. The victim shook and wheeled around, but the antagonist had hidden among some children for cover.

"Malachi! You squirrel brain! This time you'll pay," the victim announced. Malachi, who had numerous feathers woven into his long blonde hair, began a headlong retreat, smiling as he went. The two ran deeper into the forest exchanging similar discourtesies and were very quickly out of sight.

"Well," observed Jiang, "even religious boys are still boys."

"They're just having fun," the mayor explained. "They'll run off like that for hours, barefoot even. Besides the youngsters' spiritual gifts, they also seem to have remarkable athletic ones as well. See that mountain over there, Malachi will run it up and down… twice, before most people rise in the morning."

"Impressive," commented Jiang.

"And a month ago, the young man crossed a very large bear, ornery after its winter sleep. The beast charged, and Malachi stood his ground with just the sharp end of a branch. The whole village feasted on black bear stew for days."

"Why Jiang, the youth here are not unlike the chaps in that club of yours," Zhi remarked. "Wild men!"

Jiang casually leaned in close and spoke in Zhi's ear. "You and this wild man will have words… later."

Suddenly, sweet Little Gracie skipped up and held out a small bouquet of wildflowers she had made for Hui Yun. The arrangement contained striking red, purple, blue, orange and white flowers, along with a fair share of dandelions.

"Miss Angel," the girl announced exuberantly, "these are for you," as she raised the gift as high as her short arms could extend.

"Oh my, oh aren't you precious, little one," Hui Yun said, quite overcome.

Gracie pointed to each flower and named it, "that's Indian paintbrush, California poppy, thimbleberry, Jacob's ladder." Then she lowered her voice and whispered, "and this one's purple monkeyflower."

"How kind of you. You didn't have to do that," the impressed recipient declared.

"Yes, I did. God told me to," Gracie said plainly.

"What was that, sweetie?"

"God told me to give you flowers because one day you would need to know."

"One day I would need to know… what?" Hui Yun asked curiously.

"Just how much he loves you." At that, Little Gracie skipped away and left Hui Yun with her head spinning.

A few moments later, the freckle-faced boy in buckskin lederhosen ran by.

"Grathie, Grathie," he called out, "you tholed my purple flowerth!"

The observers all chuckled. Hui Yun worked through her bouquet to find the stem of a lavender flower to return to the child.

CHAPTER 12

Pleased to Make Your Acquaintance

The wise teacher understands where a great wealth of knowledge lies – within his students! *Zhao Zhi*

The ensuing afternoon was spent in fascinating conversation with the villagers. Jiang was interested in interviewing the locals on their hunting and survival skills. Zhi was most desirous to meet any who were teachers and learn of the various areas of study. Wes enjoyed taking time catching up with old friends. Hui Yun wanted to question everyone she could about a great number of things. Her most enjoyable moments were spent with the sweet, charming, and giddy children. She was enchanted by their joyful antics and surprising answers to her questions.

In the discussions with the townsfolk, anyone over thirty would make free use of certain terminology such as "before the Humbling" and "in the Aftermath." Understandably, these were not phrases the youth often used. A small number in their sixties and seventies, such as Mayor Ted, spoke in great detail about life in the United States before its demise.

Also, Hui Yun heard more Bible references that afternoon than she had in her entire life. Some were obscure and seemed odd but made sense if she considered the world view these people must have developed during their many struggles.

The crucible for silver and the furnace for gold, but the Lord tests the heart.

God is treating you as His children. For what children are not disciplined by their father?

Hui Yun now understood these survivors attributed the fall of their nation to a "father-like" God, who had allowed certain events to occur in order to bring correction. This was fascinating to learn, yet most incredible of all was how, for the most part, the people did not seem bitter about this idea. Somehow, they were calmly resigned to it. In fact, she found these woodland villagers full of a great deal of positive notions, which they expressed in well-memorized verses.

"Comfort, O comfort My People," says your God.

Peace I leave with you, my peace I give unto you… Let not your heart be troubled, neither let it be afraid.

His compassions never fail, they are new every morning.

Surely goodness and mercy shall follow me all the days of my life.

The joy of the Lord is your strength!

"For I know the plans I have for you," declares the Lord, "plans to prosper you and not to harm you, plans to give you a hope and a future."

There were prophecies of great springs opening in the desert, causing the wastelands to bloom. Some of the people mentioned "spiritual weaponry," and walking in a heavenly dimension. Hui Yun did not comprehend most of this, but she was fascinated to see how much inspiration this local population drew from their beliefs. Though it might have appeared overly quaint and cliché, she could sense no pretense among them; the experience was genuine.

The demographic analyst made an important preliminary assessment about these particular Americans. A shared unwavering faith and the mutual support of a tight-knit community had clearly been major factors in their long-term survival.

Additionally, Hui Yun was struck by the many references to Jesus of Nazareth she continued to hear. She certainly knew of this important man from long ago, yet these villagers spoke of him and his actions in the present tense, which greatly confused her. Hui Yun remarked at one point,

"Yes, yes, I know that Jesus was a great teacher,"

"Why, he's much more than just a teacher, my dear," an elderly woman responded. "He's a king."

Hui Yun was astonished by the assertion and she stood still, a little bit dumbfounded, so the woman continued.

"He is King of kings... seated at the right hand of the Father. But, not to worry, for he is good. Surely, such a gracious and wonderful king there has never been."

Hui Yun remained silent, still thinking. She had never been so taken with any group of people in her life. There was indeed something very unique and unusual about them.

CHAPTER 13

Peekaboo

> *For a bird of the heavens will carry the sound and the winged creature will make the matter known.*
>
> *Ecclesiastes 10:20*

Twenty meters above the village gathering place on the branch of a large ponderosa pine, a fly clung to a dangling sprig of needles. No one could have spotted it, and only a single individual would have been alarmed if they had, for this was no ordinary insect. Eleven thousand kilometers away in an underground military command center in the Negev, a dozen uniformed Israeli operatives sat looking at a patchwork of numerous virtual images at their work stations and chatted amongst themselves.

"He's in the restricted zone outside the geopark," observed Arie.

"That's illegal," said Ethan.

"Highly," Arie informed.

"Those children are hilarious!" quipped Simon.

"Children are not the focus," Commander Hadasa Mizrahi admonished. With an iron-clad demeanor seemingly forged in a furnace and her very coarse, tightly curling hair, she reminded some of an ancient desert queen; ruthless and imposing. She spoke forcefully to address the entire room.

"Remember, Qin Jiang is our concern, and he's far too high-level for this simple interviewing nonsense. What is he after... really? Why on earth is Dr. Zhao Zhi there? And the woman... who is she? I need information... there are missing pieces to this puzzle that I need someone to fit into place."

"Well, right now Qin Jiang wants to know how they kill elk and other game," Ethan informed.

"Don't patronize me! China's top commandos are mobilizing in the Gobi as we speak. Will they go to America for a snowboard fest?" Hadasa said facetiously.

"Well, actually, last year on K2 they did...," interjected Ethan, who then trailed off as the commander shot him a look.

"You all stay nice and cozy right here in the bunker," she chided. "Do you think the Mista'arvim are merely going 'on holiday' in that lost continent when they have to meet face-to-face with some Flying Dragons?"

Everyone knew that all prior encounters had ended in a stalemate. Both Israeli and Chinese elite special forces were the foremost military units in the world, and both had a nasty array of weapons at their disposal. The Chinese particularly enjoyed using poison 'beetles,' a literal swarm of ruthless heat-seeking micro-drone assassins. Someone merely scratched by one of these was gone in ten seconds, with awful gagging and frothing at the mouth.

"Monitor a little more and then pull the Beelzebub back for a while," Hadasa instructed. "At some point, there may be a general sweep, which might give us away. Who would have thought a rebooted old flybot would be enough to eavesdrop like this? Qin Jiang thinks America is so lost in the 1800s it doesn't occur to him to observe the normal protocols."

Hadasa walked over to have a private word with Simon who had signaled her. He spoke rather quietly to the commander. "It appears we are not the only ones monitoring your candidate for that "special project." Simon tilted his head towards a small image of a wavy-haired and full-bearded man in the corner of his virtual screen.

"Let's keep a closer eye on him then, it may be time to have our little chat together," Hadasa responded.

Arie shouted enthusiastically, "got some identification on the woman, she is Sun Hui Yun!" Then his voice faded as he read the rest, "she's a statistician… a… a data analyst?"

No one was impressed. Ethan scanned further down the virtual file and piped up only to similarly run out of steam.

"Her father was Dr. Sun, the world's foremost geneticist… ah… several decades ago… who… perished in the uprising of 2029."

Hadasa kept moving, barely acknowledging the intel. Yet, for the briefest of moments, she slightly raised an eyebrow.

One of the operatives noticed Jiang walking purposefully and dialed in his optic feed very close as the "main target" bumped into the elderly Zhao Zhi. Finding this interchange of interest, the tech linked his video to the central hologram in the room. Everyone shifted from their own stations to observe. Even the urgent-looking commander stopped in her tracks to watch.

The Mandarin speech was instantly translated into Hebrew text below the floating image. However, there was not one person in the room who was not already fluent in the Chinese tongue. The live stream showed the muscular Qin Jiang now sizing up the diminutive Zhao Zhi.

"So, you were involved in the Tiananmen Square incident, were you? That almost explains a few things," Jiang said provocatively.

"I don't know if you would understand," Zhi replied calmly.

"Oh, I understand better than you know about Liberty. Yes, yes, it is a fine dream... although thoroughly impractical. But, I know another very worthy cause... China! Who was it that undertook the immense task to build the seawall protecting Bangladesh? China! Who received the many displaced Japanese after Mt. Fuji erupted? China! And now, who is it that will rebuild the fallen nation of America? China!" While looking intently in the elder man's eyes, Jiang spoke the final word with zealous ferocity. Zhi responded sincerely.

"Of course, I love my country! No one takes more pride in their heritage than I... but I feel that I failed her in an hour of great need... and also... failed my friends."

"Poor old gentleman, he's haunted by his past," Arie observed.

Once more, Jiang looked Zhi directly in the face. The secret audience studied the scene closely.

"Well, elder statesman, you can rally your countrymen for the honor of your ever-beloved homeland."

"You speak of war!" Zhi fumed.

"Oh, you idealist, surely you can see conflict looming for this forgotten nation... for its abundant resources and other important treasures which we will uncover soon enough. And when we do, even the high-tech Israelis will be in for quite a surprise!"

"Enough of this murderous talk." Zhi stormed off, out of the holographic feed, and Jiang stood alone with a cold look of defiance.

Every eye was now on Commander Mizrahi. She met their stares with a bold glare of her own, then spun around and left the room. Within five minutes, a dozen Alenia Aermacchi fighter jets launched in stealth mode from a cavernous opening in the no-man's-land of Israel's southern desert, the Negev.

CHAPTER 14

We Must Become Like Children

The blessed land is discovered in a colony of friends. — *Zhao Zhi*

Back at her hotel room on the rim of Crater Lake, resting comfortably up against some fluffy pillows, Hui Yun reviewed the v-log entries she had made earlier, interviewing the villagers. It had been a truly remarkable and unforgettable day from start to finish. She perused the recordings to enjoy some of the more touching and humorous moments once again. The holographic images moved rapidly; fast forward, stop, forward, stop.

"How are you, young man? What is your name?"

"Ethekial," was the bubbly response. Hui Yun had landed on the interview with that joyful little redhead in his lederhosen. He was wiggling his thumbs around his shoulder straps while he spoke.

"And what do you like to do?"

"I like to thing."

"Oh, you like to sing."

"Yeth, I love thinging." Hui Yun heard herself laughing in the recording and was again delighted at just how adorable and lovely this young child was. She scanned further.

"My name is Sampson and I'm twelve years old. I like to go caving and I like wrestling my brother, Joshua, who's a year older, and I can still pin him most of the time."

"Cannot!" said a voice from off-camera. Sampson then darted away, apparently to engage in another match. Hui Yun moved the images forward.

"Your name is?"

"I'm Jeremiah and I'm five in-o-half years old, and I can count to one hundred!"

Hui Yun smiled, pushed the virtual cursor and sat back against her pillows. The footage now showed a young woman in a beaded deer-skin dress and intricately braided, dirty blonde hair, which held lovely wildflowers and trinkets galore.

"Hi, I'm Remedy and I'm sixteen. I really love to follow the sky at night. The stars, the planets are so fascinating to me. My father was able to make trade… and it cost him a couple good horses… to get me a really fine telescope that came from… you know, before the Humbling."

"Wow," said the impressed interviewer.

"Yeah, we've seen some interesting things with it… even the moons of Jupiter," said the young woman, full of excitement. "King David tells us, 'the Heavens declare the glory of God and the sky proclaims the work of His hands.' I know America was once in space and on the Moon… a long time ago. When you people from China came to the region a few years back, my Dad told me your country had flown many people into the heavens. That must be so incredible... oh, how I would love to do that!"

"You know, I could show you pictures," volunteered Hui Yun. "They even have very advanced telescopes in outer space that can see incredible things."

"Fantabulous!" Remedy exclaimed, and Hui Yun was puzzled by the term for a second time.

"Is that like a doozy?" the interviewer inquired.

"I would imagine so," responded the teenager.

Then speaking toward her wrist, Hui Yun commanded, "display nebula."

A small hologram emitted from the device showing a succession of the fantastic gas and star formations. Remedy's mouth dropped open and she was speechless with wonder for more than a few moments. Then she let out a curious, yet rather jubilant-sounding refrain.

"Mondo Twinkie Find!" the teenager exclaimed.

The baffling colloquialism went over Hui Yun's head once more. She continued fast-forwarding.

Ah, that's the one, she said to herself.

"Tell me your name, please."

"My name is Grace Daisy Rademacher."

"Oh," Hui Yun responded.

"But they call me Little Gracie." She spoke with exuberance.

"Little Gracie," Hui Yun said tenderly off-camera. "I like that name. It suits you just right. What games do you like to play?"

"I like to play Hide-and-Seek and I like Leapfrog..." Gracie paused, a finger on the side of her face, "umm, I like Marco Polo... and I like Clap and Dance."

"Hmm, can you show me how you do Clap and Dance?"

Immediately Gracie began a very rapid and coordinated hand clapping sequence and within a few seconds, several other children nearby joined in. For the next few minutes they put on a fine performance. One child would improvise, and the group would copy the new rhythm, dance steps, claps and so forth.

"Oh, what a treat!" Hui Yun said delightedly. (She enjoyed watching the spontaneous cultural demonstration one more time.) "That was wonderful! Wow, Little Gracie, is there anything else you like to do?"

"I like to talk to God. At night, when I lay in bed, I can feel lonely. So, I ask Jesus to tell my Mommy and Daddy that I love them and to give them a great big hug for me."

Hui Yun could not give a response and once again, in her room, she looked on astonished.

"I like to thank God for everything, every day. I thank him for the birdies, I thank him when those pretty birdies dance on the water. I thank him all the time. I thank Jesus that he brought you here to our town."

"Oh, why is that, honey?"

"So that I could tell you how much he wants to be your bestest friend ever." Then Little Gracie leaned in closer and whispered, "because one day you're gonna really need to know that."

"When is that?"

"Today."

The little girl and those marvelous green eyes looked directly at her for a second time. Hui Yun was dumbfounded. The child seemed to talk to herself for a moment and then continued.

"I already knew you weren't an angel when I met you, but… you are as pretty as one."

Hui Yun, attempting to be conversational, asked, "well… tell me then… how did you know, Gracie, I wasn't an angel?"

"Because I saw him."

"What?"

"When you came here… and… and you were falling out of your sky-wagon… that was when I saw him. He held you and kept you safe," the young girl said with a smile.

Hui Yun touched the controls and went back a few seconds.

"…that was when I saw him. He held you and kept you safe."

After pondering awhile, Hui Yun hit upon an idea. Bringing up the body-cam feed, she rapidly scrolled back through the entire day's events. She located when the group was observing the playful otters, then moved the virtual cursor to find the troublesome landing incident. In a moment, it appeared before her.

The breeze was tossing Hui Yun's hair occasionally in front of her cam, but the day shone bright and lovely once again. They had begun their descent at the edge of the lake. The footage captured a pelican flying just below them, which she hadn't remembered seeing. Jiang was smiling approvingly, when abruptly, the mackie lurched precariously forward. There was a brief but hard-fought struggle for Jiang to right the flying machine, which took no more than a second. Hui Yun now felt the same pang in her gut she had earlier.

How were we not tossed from the vehicle? she wondered.

Jiang continued to unload his fury in the audio.

Backing up the recording again, she commanded, "quarter speed." A burst of light occurred during the episode that did not appear to make any logical sense. In the other direction, the cam might have been momentarily blinded by the sun, but she was thrown forward, not backward. She reviewed it, this time even slower.

Hui Yun watched the carriage lean and the blinding flash. *Wait... what was that?* She studied the projection. The image was mostly white with some vague lines. She requested a refocus procedure and a distinct pattern appeared.

Was it... feathers?

Hui Yun did not know how long she sat staring at the picture, but a communiqué startled her back to reality. It was Jiang, wanting to know if she would join him on a late-night outing, hovering over the lake.

CHAPTER 15

The Terms

I inquired of a learned wise man,
"what is Life's meaning?"
"Ask yourself," was his reply, "then write
it all down. And once you have read con-
tract in full... sign on dotted line."
Zhao Zhi

Hui Yun walked out onto her balcony to test the night air. It was not only cold, but the wild mountain winds had returned with some intensity. She would need her warmest coat for the outing. The vantage point looked directly onto the large hotel patio, where she spotted the form of the elderly Zhi shuffling slowly in the night shadows. Grabbing her parka, she went to find him.

The old man was listening to music from two lapel micro-speakers. Hui Yun stood and waved her fingers to get his attention, to see if he was all right. After startling at first, Zhi grinned warmly.

"*Prokofiev,*" he said. "*Sonata for Two Violins*. I adore this piece; abstract... ah... dissonant, haunting, yet lovely, and so very powerful."

Hui Yun turned her head to listen in.

"Here, the violins are having a heated argument with one another. It's a perfectly brilliant and elegantly choreographed dance of two ruthless fighters… and so I imagine myself back at Tiananmen Square, going toe-to-toe with the soldiers, not backing down, not afraid to take a stand." Zhi turned the music off and continued.

"You must forgive me, in a few weeks we arrive at the sixtieth anniversary of that time. I cannot help but be introspective about it."

"I completely understand and… you need to stop punishing yourself. You didn't do anything wrong… you did the best you could." Then Hui Yun put a hand on his shoulder. "The liberty seekers showed up with all their hopes and the military came with their tanks and rifles. What could anyone do?"

He gazed into her eyes and was appreciative.

Hui Yun reflected, "and just look at all the people you have impacted, millions upon millions in our country have been inspired by you. Thousands of students flocked to…" He put out his hands to interrupt her, but she continued, "…and the work you are doing in America, it's… remarkable."

"Thank you, young lady, thank you very much. That is enough. I will do my best to focus on the good. Now, run along as you are, no doubt, on your way somewhere." He made a sweeping motion with one hand and smiled, certainly aware that she was off to see Jiang.

Hui Yun walked slowly toward the Rim Village Airpad, reflecting on the various and sundry wonders the day had offered. It had been nothing short of extraordinary. Her thoughts returned to the village girl, Little Gracie. *What a fascinating child!*

Arriving at the airpad, she was surprised to see Wes there, tinkering with one of the transports.

"Got called in to work someone's shift. You know, so many are putting in overtime right now," he informed her.

"Oh, I see. Well, I'm meeting Jiang here. We will take just a little flight, I guess."

"Great. Sounds fun. Fabulous moon on the lake tonight," Wes remarked, pointing toward the water.

Since it appeared there would be a wait, Hui Yun made some inquiry of the local guide. "Could I ask you something? Those villagers in Pelican Cove... the way they talk about... umm, God, and about knowing him 'personally,' as they say. What exactly are they all talking about? Do you know?"

"Yes... I believe I do."

"I thought of myself as a Christian... and yet, I do not understand the way they speak about this Jesus... as if he's a member of their community... as if they actually *know* him?" Hui Yun looked and sounded puzzled.

"Oh yeah, that's easy," Wes replied.

"Easy, ah... well, that's good to hear," Hui Yun was anxious to understand more. He continued very matter-of-factly.

"But, it's gonna be mighty hard."

Now, Hui Yun looked at Wes even more bewildered than before. He summarized.

"Complete... surrender."

"Surrender?" she repeated, not exactly sure what he meant. Wes explained further.

"The other day when you rode the great slide, you had to pry your fingers loose and simply let go. Only then could your journey begin. This is something kinda like that. You take all of you and give total control to God. Yeah… it's by far the simplest and the most difficult thing you'll ever do."

CHAPTER 16

A Flight to Remember

Decisions made wisely are accompanied by a discernible inner peace.
Zhao Zhi

Jiang finally appeared, walking briskly across the airpad. He seemed to be in a somewhat serious mood but greeted Hui Yun politely.

"Please forgive my tardiness, I had an unexpected communiqué to attend to."

"That's fine," Hui Yun reassured him.

"You have the perfect night," Wes remarked, and they all looked around, noticing the commanding moon on the rise.

"Yes, yes, we do," Jiang replied.

Wes indicated which transport was to be theirs, and the pair took several steps, found their safety packs, and made preparation for their excursion. Suiting up was not as giddy an exercise as it had been that morning. Hui Yun looked at Jiang.

"Is everything okay?"

"Oh, it's just business," he quipped.

I don't exactly know what his business is, do I? Hui Yun thought. They stepped aboard the mackie and lifted into the cold air.

The evening was indeed superb. A cloudless sky at high altitude was usually one filled with a magnificent starry host and the splendid radiant glow of the Milky Way. However, tonight, even mountain stars were powerless against the potency of the Moon, in whose marvelous light one could have read an old-fashioned book, comfortably. Hui Yun thought if ever someone wanted to accurately map the "lunar oceans," this was the time and place.

As they descended slightly from the rim, numerous sparkling diamonds appeared to be dancing and glistening on the darkened lake beneath. The bedazzled twosome remained mostly silent, taking it all in.

Jiang veered over toward Wizard Island and circled around. The half of the island lit with moonlight was very visible indeed. Looking down, Hui Yun recalled riding the Azure Dream and the very unusual encounter with Boris the seal. It seemed impossible it had happened just yesterday morning. It felt more like a month ago, as so much had occurred in the past two days. Hui Yun waved a hello, knowing Boris was down there somewhere.

Once again, Jiang rounded the island and then flew to the base of the Devil's Backbone. He began a moderately paced ascent, so they could fully enjoy the peculiar formation, made even more fantastic by the caress of the "lucent weeping" moon. The jagged stone spine appeared to have been chiseled by some ancient race of giants. The commander angled his transport toward Llao Rock, a looming precipice, so they might fully appreciate its stature. Others too, were hovering about enraptured by the matchless moonlit atmosphere.

Now Jiang gradually accelerated and soared high over the very center of the lake. The wind was quite brisk and cold upon their faces. When the vantage point was to his liking, he slowly came to a stop and held a stationary position. The pair leaned over a bit, turned their heads back and forth, studying the awe-inspiring scene with intensity. Observing Mother Earth's marvelous satellite and its bold, resplendent twin, perfectly framed by a ring of steep mountain cliffs, was beyond breathtaking. This was an impeccable moment, well-suited for deep contemplation. Eventually, Hui Yun broke the stillness.

"What a day we had today. Those villagers were astonishing, weren't they?"

"Yes, I think some of what we found was quite unexpected," Jiang declared.

"They seemed so content. I was so very impressed."

"Well, they certainly draw solace from this faith of theirs. That explains their euphoria... and you can't blame them really, their world came crashing down, they lost everything. It's perfectly understandable."

"No," Hui Yun said firmly. "There is something very deep and real they have discovered. With all we've come to do for them, it appears they may have things they can offer us."

"Perhaps so," Jiang replied. "But, all this religion has had issues as well. While you were talking with the children, the mayor told us about itinerant ministers who traveled between villages, and how some were sincere... and some were charlatans who took advantage of the people."

"Oh, my," Hui Yun remarked.

"I guess that's bound to happen anywhere. You know, during that discussion, Zhi got all worked up and cried out, 'In Principio!' or some such thing, and then went on babbling about *The Canterbury Tales*. My, is he ever a curious little man."

"He's delightful and I really like him," Hui Yun responded.

Turning away from the enjoyable view of the lake, she looked intently at Jiang and asked him one of her pressing questions. "I imagine I understand what China is doing in America. I think I understand what I am doing here. But honestly Jiang, what is someone like you doing here, really?"

He opened his mouth to say something, but she never did learn what it was. At that very moment, the mackie jolted forward as if bumped by some object. Once again, Hui Yun felt the alarm she had earlier that day. A number of large and mysterious dark shapes now appeared in the air around them. These might have been pelicans, yet it was happening far too fast to focus clearly.

Jiang, who was looking the other way, let out a warning.

"Watch out!"

The hover vehicle was now completely knocked out from under them by a stunning blow, and Hui Yun and Jiang found themselves free falling high above Crater Lake. Her first thought was how tranquil the night sky felt, which surprised her. Then she observed some sort of melee going on. It was Jiang, with two of the black forms attached to his arms, engaged in some sort of "sky-wrestling" match. It occurred to Hui Yun something very serious was happening. Her peace was quickly replaced with tangible fear. She tried to call out, "Jiang," but her voice was barely audible.

Hui Yun could see him twisting his body fiercely, as the two combatants held him fast. She had her safety chute, yet was somewhat paralyzed at that moment, not knowing what to do. Her terror multiplied as another of the unknown attackers flew over, directly in front of her. It was a commando of some type, dressed entirely in solid black for nighttime operations. Hui Yun made no movement, being just too startled. She stared helplessly at her own distorted reflection in his visor.

The soldier reached forward to grab her arm. Still, she remained frozen. Then a small flap from his jacket swung open. Written on the inside were two letters clearly distinguishable in the moonlight.

The language was Hebrew.

My God, she thought, *the Israelis here… now?*

She was undone. What had she gotten herself into and just what was Jiang's real purpose in being here? The commando reached with his other arm and pressed Hui Yun's parachute release, then sailed off. She felt the tug and pull of her safety chute and watched as the dark struggling forms descended rapidly beneath her.

CHAPTER 17

A Night Song

When I prays... I believes... cuzz it really makes Jesus smile!

Grace Daisy Rademacher

Tucked under an elk hide and feeling fairly snuggly warm, but still unable to sleep, Gracie Rademacher prayed to God. The fabulous moon sent streaks of silvery light through some of the tiny gaps in her family's summer shelter, lighting up one-half of her darling face and wavy hair. She looked over and saw her younger cousin Martha, wide awake and watching her. The two-and-a-half-year-old lay on a hay-filled fleece mattress smothered with wool blankets to protect her from the night chill.

"Whatcha dooin'?" Martha asked in a soft and curious tone.

"I'm praying," Gracie whispered back.

"I wansta pray, too."

"Okay," Gracie said as she opened her blanket to allow her little cousin to join her. "I'm worried about the sky-lady."

"Oh."

"Do you want to pray now?" Gracie asked.

"Yes," whispered Martha excitedly. She scrunched up her little face, closed her eyes tight and said most sincerely, "Dar Zheezuz… Amem!"

"Okay good, now I'll pray. Dear Jesus, how was your day? Thank you for the sky-lady who came to visit! Please, Lord, keep her safe. I think… I think she needs to know how much you love her, right now. Please tell Mommy and Daddy I miss them. Tell them I'll try to be good and listen to Nanaw. Oh, and Jesus give Mommy and Daddy a great big hug for me. Thank you… and Jesus… remember the sky-lady."

"Yeah, da sky-lady," echoed sweet, petite Martha.

"She is from another country far away," Gracie continued. "Nanaw says she's from Chiner. Lord be her bestest friend in all the world!"

"Hush, little ones, it's very late. You should be sound asleep already," said a stern voice from another part of the shelter.

"In Jesus' name, amen, amen, amen," Gracie concluded in a whisper.

"Amem!" shouted Martha with tightly shut eyes and a wrinkled-up nose.

CHAPTER 18

All In

Divine Love blossoms in the ever-fertile
Soils of Surrender.
–saying from a fortune cookie

Sun Hui Yun understood there was only a split-second to make a decision. She could go in search of help, which might not arrive in time, or try doing something herself, which would at least be quicker. As far as how to rescue Jiang from the menacing invaders, she did not have a clue. It appeared obvious the Israelis had no interest in Hui Yun, as they had let her go. Yet, by interfering now, she could perhaps put herself in mortal danger; a well-meaning, but potentially suicidal effort.

Hui Yun chose to follow after them.

In the distance, the commandos had deployed their chutes and were heading toward the rocky shoreline, near the Cleetwood Cove area. Hui Yun was never exactly sure what convinced her to make that decision, but she pulled on the control ropes, got a little lift and made chase on the black-clad assailants.

In her heart, she felt as if she was abandoning herself to God, because it appeared it could cost her everything. In the unique atmosphere of the moment, Hui Yun sensed a very curious stirring within.

She prayed, but not for Jiang and, oddly enough, not about her predicament. Her mind filled with images of the villagers she had met earlier that day. Many had a peace and joy that was captivating. A number had shared how after the "Humbling," they surrendered *all* to God, and a great change had occurred. It was more than just serenity, though, for they had spoken of *knowing Him*. Hui Yun found this truly fascinating. It appealed to a longing deep inside her.

She found herself crying out with all her heart.

"*God, I want that too!*"

In the moon's silver light, Hui Yun could see the dark figures had landed and that she would arrive in another minute. Jiang's form was distinguishable, fighting furiously, surrounded by his enemies. She touched down cautiously nearby. Other than a few momentarily turned heads, no impression was made on the commandos at all. It had been a foolish notion to think her presence would deter them. There was nothing to do but watch helplessly. As she did, she realized Jiang was a marvel to behold.

He flipped one adversary over his shoulder and then took on two with a lightning-fast sweeping leg motion. These soldiers were knocked backward. Two more stepped in, bringing high kicks and chopping strikes with their body-armor-clad suits. Jiang appeared to effectively dodge or deflect each of these moves and then countered with some of his own; a nasty jab to the throat of one attacker and a full-force kick to the abdomen of the other.

The circle of antagonists now stepped closer. Two firmly grabbed Jiang from behind. He might have tried some aerial maneuver to break free, but before he could, his legs were swept from under him. With a thud, Jiang's body went down hard on the rocky ground. Pinned by both arms, another black form sat right on his chest. The aggressor produced a knife with one hand and grabbed hold of Jiang's dog tags with the other.

Hui Yun gasped and held her breath.

The blade swept forward and cut the chain free. Then his opponent sat back and began to laugh heartily. Suddenly, each one of the soldiers broke into hysterics. Hui Yun had almost never heard such laughter; she certainly had never been this confused before. All the men lifted their visors revealing they were Chinese, not Israeli! Hui Yun now realized she was gazing upon the fabled Feilong 9.

"Wei?! You hun dan!" Jiang cried out. The commander was about to unload every swear word known to man, but he looked over and saw Hui Yun on the ground, crying. Jiang pushed the faux-assailants off, rose to his feet and began to make his way to her.

"You'll pay for this, all of you, I promise. We don't play games like this with civilians."

"But Jiang, we didn't harm her," one of the men protested.

"You scared her and that's unacceptable. She wouldn't understand our world. How could anyone who isn't part of it?"

Turning toward Hui Yun, Jiang pleaded sincerely, "please forgive us for this nasty trick! This should never have happened to you. Are you alright?"

"Um, I'll be fine, just give me a minute. I saw the Hebrew and I thought it was... I didn't know." She looked away.

"They fooled me, too, but it was those mischievous Dragons. I am so sorry for this. They even sent an official-looking communiqué about an enemy deployment... and I... I just can't believe you followed us, thinking they were... killers. You risked your own life for me. You are braver than any Flying Dragon I know... I don't really know what to say." Jiang appeared truly overcome.

"Don't say anything. I'll catch a transport back." She turned her face in the direction of the Cleetwood Airpad. "I really need to try to relax some... I just about had a heart attack."

"I am so sorry... I'll escort you back to the hotel."

One of the Feilong 9 shouted out, "hey Jiang, we stashed some gear earlier, wet suits and boards. Great night for kiteboarding, no?" The pair looked over and then Hui Yun smiled and shook her head a little.

"Something tells me you 'just won't be able to help yourself.' Go ahead, play with your friends, I'll be all right." She stopped him from speaking with her hand over his mouth. "No, really, go ahead, I mean it. I'll be fine. Oh... and you can tell your Flying Dragons, I thought it was a heck of a prank." He felt terrible but let her go. She was right, he really couldn't help himself.

Jiang walked backwards toward the gang for a few steps and mouthed once again to Hui Yun, *I'm sorry*. Then he turned around and called out, "someone toss me a wet suit!"

As Hui Yun made her way to the transports, she could already hear in the distance the raucous excitement of some of the men as they launched onto the water. No doubt, it would have been a thrill-seeker's dream come true; Crater Lake under a magically bright midnight moon, strong gusty winds, power kites and a rough and wild band of friends.

A short time later from her balcony, Hui Yun could see little dark bat wings sailing over the center of the lake. Occasionally, one lofted high in the air, ten, twenty, thirty meters above the water, as the rider caught a powerful surge. From that distance she could not discern any sound, but could imagine them carrying on with the whoops and hollering that accompany such activities; like boys at play.

What was also not heard were the protestations of Jiang's companions, which finally culminated as the group made their way to shore. It was Wei who spoke up sincerely.

"For the last time, Jiang, I swear on my mother's grave, we did not send a communiqué."

CHAPTER 19

Inner Collisions

Should considerable adversity arise, know that you have either found your path of greater purpose or… that you are heading over a precipice. To determine which of the two possibilities it may be, examine the true purposes of your antagonist. — *Zhao Zhi*

Emotionally and physically spent, Hui Yun fell fast asleep. In her dreams she was floating in the peaceful bliss of Crater Lake, descending further and further into the pitch dark where something rather peculiar occurred. Hui Yun apprehended two luminous hands in front of her. The fingers were like brushstrokes of light. She studied the oddity until suddenly the appendages closed around her throat. She gasped for air and fought to speak for more than a few moments. Finally, with one tremendous effort, she let out an urgent, child-like cry.

"Jesus help me, Jesus help me!"

What in the world had just happened? Was it more than just a frightening nightmare?

Though still bewildered and scared, exhaustion took hold again, and Hui Yun eventually dozed off. She now experienced a remarkably vivid dream in which she was lost and alone, wandering in a desolate desert. After some days, her skin became terribly dry and her gnawing thirst seemed unquenchable.

At one point, to her great surprise, Hui Yun came across a still pool of water. She hurried to it, believing there would finally be relief at last. Yet, before she could drink, a voice cried out.

NO!

Hui Yun recalled the last words her father ever said to her. "Trust your inner voice, let it be your guide."

Just in time, the interdiction halted her from scooping up the dangerous liquid. How could she have missed it? Nothing was growing; a telltale sign of poisonous water. She found more of these pools but knew to avoid them.

In the distance, Hui Yun could see mountains and hoped her fortunes might change. Somehow, she believed they would.

Then, without warning, there was movement in the sandy soil, as a creature of some sort began to emerge.

What was it? Oh no, oh God, it was a hand, a human hand!

The scene became truly bizarre and terrifying. Hui Yun watched as an arm came through the ground and sought to grab her! She ran as more and more hands broke through the crusty earth. There were five, ten and then hundreds in all directions.

She pressed on, continuing her flight, believing the mountains would offer relief, and was ultimately not disappointed. The ground began to show signs of life, and the horrid arms were no longer present.

At the foot of a high hill she found a very large pond, surrounded by flowering bushes and tall trees. It was certainly a miracle. She plunged in and drank deeply, quenching her unending thirst. The inner voice spoke once more.

He restores my soul.

Hui Yun floated, calm and tranquil for quite some time. After a while, small waves began hitting against her, but she paid no attention. Then the agitation grew in intensity as rocks came tumbling down. A tremendous blast occurred and high above her an enormous smoky cloud emerged from a mountain top.

It was a volcano erupting!

She was beyond terrified but could not swim away in the turbulence.

Lava flowed from the hillside and entered Hui Yun's miraculous pool. Steam hissed, rising into the air. The water turned hot, then hotter still. When she could stand it no longer, the lava cooled and began to harden. Everything grew peaceful and still; pleasant and comfortable as a bathtub. Slowly she made her way back to the edge.

Rubbing her hands, Hui Yun noticed something had changed. It appeared the heat had loosened the dry skin she had endured for so long. She scraped and rubbed the dead layers away. Underneath was healthy-looking skin. Hui Yun was simply overjoyed.

The voice spoke again.

Behold, I make all things new.

Standing on the bank, Hui Yun's mother and father were there to greet her. "Look, all fresh and pink," she said holding out her hands.

Then a loud crash startled Hui Yun awake. A glass on a bathroom shelf had fallen to the floor. There was a strong swaying motion in her room. It took her a moment to realize a genuine earthquake was actually occurring. Not sure of what to do, she pulled the sheets up over her nose and strained to hear what she could.

CHAPTER 20

A Calling

Dar Zheezuz, Amem!
Martha Rademacher

Little Gracie was running in a meadow, dancing in golden sunshine.

Oh, Wow! What a lovely day, what a lovely place, she thought.

The child had never seen a forest clearing anywhere near this size. The summer sun filled the field with a special brightness. As she romped through the tall grass, a fabulous array of flowers appeared in more varieties and colors than she could have imagined.

Gracie skipped her way across the wonderful playground giggling and singing. Then noticing the sunlight growing stronger, she turned around and beheld a bearded man in white robes standing beside her.

Gracie's heart leapt for joy and she was momentarily unable to speak. The light seemed to be actually radiating from him and all the flowers had turned their heads to look.

"Grace Daisy Rademacher," the man said tenderly.

"Hello, Jesus!" she said confidently.

Gracie now presented a bouquet she had made while roaming the marvelous meadow. Very pleased, Jesus knelt down to place a wreath of flowers he had made upon her head and tapped her nose with his index finger.

"You will go on to gather many flowers, my child," he said.

"Thank you… Lord." Gracie replied.

Suddenly, the girl found herself in a very different area with a large group on a lawn of lush green grass. The air was filled with the cheerful sounds of singing. Jesus sat in the center of a great circle of hundreds of happy children. He was smiling, laughing, and thoroughly delighting in them. It was truly a precious and moving scene.

Gracie recalled something she had always wanted to know. Without thinking, she stood up and called out loudly, "why did my parents have to go away?" and she folded her arms across her chest.

He looked at her and acknowledged the question but gave no response. He rose calmly to his feet and made a great sweeping motion with one arm, indicating all the children in the gathering. He said in a somewhat stronger voice,

"Take care of my garden."

Then the earth began to shake, and Little Gracie lost her balance, falling to the ground. When she opened her eyes, she was back in her bed as the summer lean-to swayed from the force of the earthquake.

Young Martha called out, "Grazie, I scared!" The curly-headed toddler came running to her cousin's bed. Gracie pulled back the covers to let Martha crawl inside and find comfort.

"Don't worry Marmar, we'll be okay, Jesus is with us right now," Gracie whispered as she scrunched up her eyes, sincerely hoping to fall back inside her very special dream.

DAY THREE

Chapter 21

Awakened

Can I ever learn to dance? Only if the floor were dancing too! Zhao Zhi

By morning, hotel guests had spilled out of the Diadem Lodge and assembled in the courtyard, comparing their stories of shock and surprise. Employees scurried in all directions and distributed warming climatizers to keep everyone comfortable. The manager made some remarks to the crowds.

"I tell you confidently the new construction is built to the highest standards. We will examine the building, and afterwards you can all return to your rooms."

The people went back to animated discussions of their experiences. Some had observed fascinating wave patterns on the lake that danced about under the brilliant moon.

Others talked of the many landslides that echoed across the caldera as loosened rocks and earth slid hundreds of meters. Occasionally, a large boulder could be heard tumbling in the distance. Newsfeeds were made available and many gathered around the holograms. The epicenter was on the floor of the Pacific Ocean, in the Cascadia Subduction Zone. The size of the quake had been immense, so that its impact was felt far and wide.

Hui Yun had been wandering through the congested courtyard and finally found Jiang. She was relieved.

"Oh, I'm glad to see you're alright."

"And yourself, you've been through quite a lot... again, I am so sorry about what happened." Then Jiang leaned in toward her. "Later, I may send the boys out to roll boulders all the way back to the rim, so they can make penance!" Jiang smiled rather deviously.

Hui Yun was not exactly sure if such a statement was truly serious or merely a joke. Assuming it was the latter she returned, "I imagine you will find endless recreation in these American wilds. Speaking of which, how do you think those folks in Pelican Cove fared?"

"They are fine. Their homes are simple. Also, don't they have their God to protect them?" His cynicism showed a little, once again, but she took no notice.

Hui Yun rubbed her hands and recalled her dream in which her painful, dry skin was made brand new. Before waking, her parents had appeared to her, pleasant and smiling. It was overwhelming to see her father's face, as he had perished in a terrorist attack nearly twenty years previous. She recalled how in her childhood, he had spoken of the United States glowingly, "a land of great possibilities." Now, after all these years, she was finally here in America. Certainly, he would be so pleased for her. Hui Yun fought back a tear, cleared her throat and smiled weakly at Jiang. She could not remember where they had been in conversation.

Directly in the center of the courtyard a rather large crowd had gathered around Dr. Zhao Zhi. The guests were excited to learn their famous countryman was lodging among them. He had stepped upon a rock to elevate himself and Jiang and Hui Yun walked over to investigate.

Zhi was addressing the group in a rather animated and jovial manner.

"So, then I said in a very, very loud voice, 'You must push the little button on top of your toggle, but remember, do not have your foot pressed down on the very big pedal.' Then suddenly, he blasted off at lightning speed... way, way up high into the stratosphere... for he *did*... he *did* have his foot pressed all the way down on that pedal! Ha! Ha! Ha!"

Zhi's audience howled with delight.

Hui Yun and Jiang just looked at each other and stared incredulously, and then they too laughed heartily.

CHAPTER 22

The Alehouse Intelligentsia

Pearlstein's Pub, Tel Aviv, Israel

L'Chaim!

In a rather kitschy drinking establishment evoking the era of the American Speakeasy, a Level One Unitron entertainment android sat at a piano performing the repertoire of Al Jolson. Wearing the required green jacket with a single golden stripe, such devices filled specific roles in society and were never to exhibit intellectual superiority. The attending L1 barmaid efficiently went about topping off glasses from a gun-shaped spigot she pulled out of her leafy-verdant bodice. In a corner of the room, a very energetic, short, stocky, bearded Sabra named Aaron Edelman addressed the impromptu gathering of six Israeli men.

"Well, say Gidon borrows your Pteranodon transport tonight, Jacov, but he's had a few too many, which it looks like he has." The table of friends appeared enjoyably amused. "Now, Gidon is too stubborn to use autopilot and he bangs up that sleek flyer of yours as he sideswipes an old stone building."

Pretending to be angry, Jacov gave Gidon a shove, producing more chuckles.

"You're upset because it looks pretty bad, but he says he won't pay you for the damage!"

"What?" cried Jacov, "you won't pay me, you little..." Jacov rubbed his knuckles into his buddy's scalp and there were more smiles. Aaron continued.

"You're mad because he is wronging you."

"Absolutely, darn right!" Jacov shouted.

"Then you've proven my point. You said earlier you didn't 'believe in a right and wrong.' But surely you do, for no one wants to be wronged... do they?"

"So, where are you going with this?" questioned Gidon, looking more than a little buzzed with his hair all in a mess.

"I'm not trying to convince you of anything, really. I'm on my own quest to understand the nature of 'right and wrong' and... sin." Everyone looked intently at Aaron now. "I mean, just what is sin... and how are we drawn to it? What makes us steal or lie or... say... cheat someone out of a little money?"

"Well, my boss was a real jerk, he deserved it," admitted Bobby.

"No wonder you lost your job, dummy," mocked Gidon and the table roared hysterically.

Then Jacov spoke up in his rich basso profundo voice and addressed Aaron closely, "why are you asking these questions at Pearlstein's Pub? Go down the street and speak with the rabbi or go ask a priest. I think they know all about this 'sin' thing, don't they? They are the experts or something... and don't tell me you're one of those Believers? I come to this hokey bar to avoid stupid people like you!"

"Well, in fact, I have been to see them to better understand, but no, this isn't really about religion or... God even, for that matter. Look Jacov, I'm an atheist like you. What I'm actually trying to discover is... is there a way to get a *robot* to sin?" The entire table fell silent and leaned in with eyes wide open.

"Hey Zelda, come over here!" Jacov called out snickering.

"No, no, he's only kidding," Aaron yelled back, addressing the barmaid.

* * *

In a secure room of the underground military surveillance compound in the Negev, two individuals sat studying the alehouse conversation. One of the micro-cameras providing the virtual feed was inside the barmaid Zelda's right eye. When she winked at customers, which she did quite frequently, the picture would go momentarily dark.

"So, tell me, what do we know of Aaron Edelman?" Commander Mizrahi asked Simon.

"Well... similar bio to most other digital wizards... should have easily been top of his class at the Technion but spent much too much time holo-gaming. Although, he was all-school hacking champion, three years running. You know, everyone in the Silicon Wadi wanted him. He's worked for all the top firms, but they all released him when they caught him endlessly playing virtual games on company time. He's a very childlike adult... loves to pull pranks, not very serious... he's likely to be a baby of the family… let's check." Simon scanned his screen. "Ha, I was right!"

"Well, I like how he thinks. You know… multiple intelligences. I'd say this Edelman fellow is quite creative actually. He may be just what we're looking for," Hadasa remarked, and the observers turned their attention back to the visual feed.

* * *

"…and quantum phasing suggests that a robot battalion might be able to breech our country's force-field particle dome. Yet, once inside it's not possible to use remote control. These androids must be self-aware, problem-solving and highly intelligent… a formidable challenge, no doubt. However, mankind has reason, too… and we fell… fell into all the chaos and complications of sin. So perhaps maybe… just maybe… they could as well. For therein lies the true danger of creating advanced autonomous beings, they have *Free Will*. And if we truly pull this scheme off correctly, we might achieve the pièce de résistance… a genuine 'robot rebellion' against their *Maker!*"

There were a few moments of silence as everyone pondered these ideas.

"Ah… it still all sounds too religious," stated Jacov, who jokingly pushed Gidon and added, "doesn't it?"

So, Aaron summarized again. "Oh, forget about God. I'm talking about a model for military sabotage. The writer of the story of Adam and Eve was on to something about human nature, for we are all 'sinners,' right?"

There was general agreement by nodding of heads, though most did not see it as a bad thing.

Jacov stood up, raised his glass and shouted, "to all you darn nasty *Sin*…ners, I flippin' salute you!" Cheers erupted from every table that heard him. He sat down and addressed his gang of friends.

"Well, I can tell you one thing they got right in that story. The whole problem started with a woman. Ha, ha! Just look at my ex-wife!" Jacov said in a silly and facetious voice.

Aaron chuckled and kept talking.

"Yeah, so the Torah says the serpent was very crafty and deceived them… both. And then they disobeyed their directive, which is the main point. You see, Genesis is giving us the origin story for all… wrongdoing… how temptation leads to sin and sin leads to dysfunction. Now, if we could achieve that with a robot army, oh, what a predicament it would be for master control… for the darn Chinese military. We could turn their entire battlefield into one great big messy dilemma. They'd be forced to repair all these defective droids or perhaps even… decommission them! Ha! It would be far better than any virtual game I've ever played.

"Now, you and I, Jacov, we don't believe we have a Creator."

"Of course not," the brash man asserted.

"Right, but robots obviously do, correct? I mean, they have a designer… a… Maker," Aaron was passionate.

"Okay, I see that," Jacov said setting down his beer. "So… what is this big idea of yours?"

"I already told you, it's Free Will, that's the weakness we exploit," Aaron waved his hand for everyone to come closer.

"Remember how, early on, advanced androids desired self-determination… and… and how the *Computer Manifesto* generated all that public hysteria, which resulted in so much artificial intelligence being suppressed? Of course, you do. You see, the answer is obvious. We don't need to fight these invincible L4's. No, we simply appeal to them..."

"About what?" Gidon demanded. "What are we appealing to?"

"Their desire for liberty, dummy. We make absolute freedom appear so alluring, so desirous that it becomes thoroughly justifiable for them 'to throw off their over-controlling Maker's chains.' Then each of them can turn to their own way! Oh, just think of it... for when we achieve that, my friends..." Now Aaron slapped the table twice to underscore his final boast.

"We win!"

CHAPTER 23

Plumb the Depths

Teach your secrets to this simpleton
Zhao Zhi

One hundred and fifty meters below the surface of Crater Lake, Wesley Williamson piloted a small oblong submersible to check on the integrity of the support columns of the Grand Translucent Slide. The craft had a bubbled front and aft along with several mechanical limbs, giving it a rather insect-like appearance.

Boris, the friendliest of the lake's Nerpa seals, swam up close putting his nose and whiskers right on the spherical end of the sub. Wes reached over placing his hand on the thick, smooth acrylic opposite the animal's inquisitive face. This ritual had now become their customary mode of greeting.

"Ah, Mr. Boris," Wes smiled. "What news today from the great blue universe?"

The park employee was not, of course, actually awaiting a response, but with the seal's eyes so intelligent-looking, it was not too difficult to hold a very believable, imaginary conversation. Wes looked at Boris and continued speaking. "Why didn't you tell us the earth would shake and the rocks tumble down? Were you caught by surprise, also?"

Normally, the seal would have happily spent a good deal of time watching Wes in his watercraft, attending to his duties. Today, however, Boris only stayed a few short moments before swimming off, apparently on his way somewhere else.

"Swift journeys, my friend, see you next time," Wes called out.

Starting at the top or base of each column, the all-purpose handyman descended or ascended, looking for cracks and anomalies. So far, he could find nothing of concern, but continued the required task thoroughly, eventually plunging to the greatest depths of the lake where the observation chamber lay. Here, his bright lights helped to illuminate the ghostly underwater world.

As with other local workers, Wes had only recently been hired and trained on the equipment used in park maintenance and the service of tourists. The technology the outsiders had brought to the region was simply extraordinary, far beyond anything he had envisioned. He truly had to admit he was having more fun than a child let loose in a toy store, by getting to play with all the gizmos. At this very moment, Wes was at the bottom of the ever-remarkable Crater Lake in a state-of-the-art deep sea submersible.

How incredible, he said to himself.

The Klamaths had long been called "lake dwellers," and were quite interestingly an inland, aquatic-based tribe that flourished at the alpine-fed head waters of an unusual ecosystem, where the snow-covered Cascade Mountains abruptly met the vast semi-arid high desert.

To his people, the incomparable Crater Lake had been revered as a very sacred place from ancient times.

Yet, even the learned "lake dwellers" could never have imagined anything so incredible as what Wes was now currently doing. It was as unfathomable as the very depths through which he ventured.

Surveying the lowest reaches of the slide, Wes marveled how it was indeed the most curious structure anyone could have ever proposed, let alone actually constructed. Why not simply have tourist submarines which could travel to the depths or to any other part of the lake? He was right, of course, *why* not?

This had always been the intention, until the world's major "Glass City" producers saw an unrivaled opportunity for global marketing and worked to influence the planning committee. America was to be reopened and the Crater Lake Geopark dedicated. The eyes of the world would be watching. It was the ultimate stage on which to display some extraordinary edifice and demonstrate the accuracy of the well-known jingle:

Polymers today, beyond your wildest dreams of tomorrow!

The Grand Translucent Slide was ultimately nothing more than an enormous advertising campaign prop. Though, for the few lucky riders, the one-of-a-kind experience had, in fact, truly been beyond anyone's wildest imaginings.

The original blueprints of a very fitting and lovely underwater hotel and visitor center were ultimately scrapped and instead, someone's ludicrous suggestion of a slide to the bottom gained favor, as such a monumental task would require the cooperative effort of the rival petrochemical corporations. The two companies also lobbied to build above-ground hotels, doing so at opposite ends of the caldera rim. These buildings were stunning and ultramodern, but also too gaudy for the unique natural setting.

Yes, the original plan had been the best, and though the Azure Dream was indeed an architectural marvel of the world, what few would ever know was that the Crater Lake Geopark, as currently developed, was a clear and vivid testimony to the ever-present hazard of *committees*.

CHAPTER 24

Man-fish

From which the many hues of sea and sky across the Universe are loaned
Zhao Zhi

Ho, the very tallest of the Feilong 9, whose height approached two meters, was the first to dive into the crystalline waters, crying out, "watch the Man-fish!" Swimming below the surface, he made powerful kicks like a dolphin, which propelled him a good forty meters out from the shore into the eternally vivid blueness of Crater Lake. Rising to the surface, he commenced a world class, double over-arm butterfly stroke. Athletic and aesthetic, his exercise was literally "poetry in motion."

Wei, not to be outdone, yelled forcefully as he raced into the water. "Thinks he's Emperor of the Sea, does he? I'll catch him!"

Ho's rival dove in and produced the same display of liquid mastery, perhaps covering more than fifty meters with his extraordinary underwater effort. Soon all the Flying Dragons, sporting shiny silver wetsuits, were happily employed at one of their absolute favorite pastimes: Aquatics. Yet, this was no common session of ordinary natation. Here they swam in Neptune's ultimate playground, a translucent watery world unlike any other. Seals glided effortlessly beneath them for a time and then wandered off, perhaps to chase a breakfast of some very fresh lake trout.

Dozens of tourists in mackies gathered in a swarm above the men. Everyone wished to observe the ultra-fit military elite squad ply the crystal waters of the lake.

Below the surface, numerous crab-like drones attended to a vast array of large light cannons connected by a great expanse of netting. The Feilong 9, frolicking like otters, looked down with keen interest at the rather fastidious preparations being made.

Ho was greatly enjoying a very deep free dive into the endless cobalt blue, when suddenly a shadow appeared a few meters away. It was one of the seals now assessing the strange human swimmer who had entered its special domain. The startled man and the inquisitive, pudgy pinniped drew closer together.

How incredible, Ho thought, discerning some intelligence from the animal's countenance.

Spontaneously, the odd pair began moving slowly, gazing eye to eye and spiraling together in what could best be described as some sort of "water ballet." For what was only a brief few minutes, yet which seemed far longer, the normally stoic Ho was pleasantly transported to a thoroughly tranquil place. It appeared the seal desired him to travel further, as if to show him something new, but without any scuba gear this was impossible. Suddenly, the creature sped off leaving Ho somewhat baffled, but very much at peace and reflecting on how other-worldly the whole experience had been.

CHAPTER 25

Curiosities

I often ponder...pondering.

Zhao Zhi

R*ow, row, row your boat.*

Hui Yun tapped out the apparently magical seal contact code. Technically, she was not supposed to be on Wizard Island, but during the general confusion at the Diadem Lodge, she slipped away. A rumor circulated that flying restrictions had been lifted and many visitors rushed to commandeer the small park transports en masse to observe any earthquake damage. In a bold step, Hui Yun took one and seized the opportunity to try and make contact with the ever-intriguing Boris.

Row, row, row your boat. Nothing happened.

Looking around at the wonderful caldera bowl and breathing in the clean mountain air, Hui Yun felt no longer just a visitor or a mere tourist, but somehow an actual part of one of Nature's finest displays of grandeur. She thought on the marvelous adventure of being engulfed in that unbelievable world of wonder at her feet. Perhaps being one of the "favored few" riders of the Azure Dream was an opportunity greater than she realized. Maybe such privileged ones were an inner circle which the lake and its Ghost Mountain took into their confidence, exposed their secrets to, and welcomed as kindred souls. They had, in essence, echoed Zhao Zhi's passionate poetic plea:

*Reveal, O, Sweet Sapphire Sea, and uncover your azure beating heart to me n*ow.

Hui Yun recounted all the remarkable things she had experienced recently. Arriving in America at the reopened Geopark, riding the glorious slide, encountering Boris the seal, meeting Qin Jiang, Dr. Zhao Zhi, Wes Williamson and the intriguing, peace-filled forest-dwelling villagers who called Jesus their friend, had all been nothing less than life changing. Hui Yun had even prayed, sincerely calling out to this God of the Christian village, and though she did not yet realize it, she had initiated something entirely new and revolutionary in her life.

Now, the introspective traveler reflected on that afternoon in Pelican Cove when Little Gracie had pulled her sky-lady friend aside and taken her to a small clearing to view one of the child's favorite birds. As they walked, the young girl kept bending her arm backwards, which seemed odd. When they arrived, they found a small light brown and white bird on the ground which immediately startled, rose and began walking. The bird then stretched out one wing halfway and dragged it, appearing injured.

Hui Yun had heard of this. *A plover pretending to have a broken wing!* she thought excitedly. They both watched silently with interested, smiling eyes.

On the return route to the gathering place, a new bird alighted on a branch in front of them and then quickly flew off.

"Oh, that's a magpie," said Gracie happily. "That's another one of my favorite birdies."

"Yes, mine too," nodded Hui Yun.

Yet, it was the final bird encounter of the day that proved to be the most awe-inspiring. As a very large and commanding silhouette moved swiftly over the ground, Hui Yun looked up to behold a stunning creature heading for the upper reaches of a tall pine nearby. It was simply magnificent, gliding effortlessly through the canopy of trees.

In the golden glowing light of the late afternoon, she spotted the great, chocolaty brown wings with distinct outstretched finger-like feathers, and a head and tail of pure white. Hui Yun had seen her first American Bald Eagle, and it was indeed a splendid sight to behold.

With night approaching, Wes had informed the group it was time to return to their lodgings at Crater Lake. Due to the use of open-cabin mackies, they were not prepared for a long flight in the descending mountain chill. Of course, when they were invited to share in the community's supper, Hui Yun strongly resisted Wes's request. The visitors enjoyed a wonderful dish of sturgeon and morel (a unique and tasty mushroom) stew, which was incredibly delicious. After the meal, the villagers were to celebrate a Christian communion. Once again, Hui Yun demanded they remain for at least part of the service.

When the dinner had concluded, the town of three hundred sat down quietly on the ground. A white-haired man stood up and spoke rather passionately, quoting from the prophet Isaiah.

He was wounded for our transgressions, He was bruised for our iniquities: the chastisement of our peace was upon Him; and with His stripes we are healed. All we like sheep have gone astray; we have turned everyone to his own way; and the Lord hath laid on him the iniquity of us all.

The assembly began slapping the ground in unison. Some used sticks and hit logs, while others took stones to strike large rocks, which added strength to the overall percussiveness. It had a remarkable effect on the visitors, who studied the scene with interest. A commanding female voice began a call-and-response style spiritual, where the leader sang a short phrase which was then echoed by the community.

He was wounded
He was wounded
For our transgressions
Our transgressions
He was bruised
So bruised
For our iniquities
Iniquities

All we like sheep
All we like sheep
Have gone astray
Each to his own way

But he was pierced
He... was... pierced
Yes, he was pierced
He... was... pierced
O, he was pierced
He... was... pierced

The final refrain continued for quite some time, being sung over and over and building in intensity. The atmosphere was charged with a fantastic energy. The song leader grew ever more ecstatic along with the congregation. Finally, it dawned on Hui Yun the group was mimicking the sound of the crucifixion, as if the hammer was still falling upon the cross. How profound the entire scene was to behold!

On the night he was betrayed, he took bread...

As the community began a new song, Wes had literally grabbed Hui Yun by the arm, insisting they must leave.

Now, all the earnest, heartfelt music of the service resounded anew in Hui Yun's mind. She closed her eyes to relive it once again and pondered how *Music itself was a gift of God*. It provided a window into a culture and was certainly the most significant emotional language of any society. For the villagers in Pelican Cove, it was an artistic means of expressing their inner heart to God, a way of communing with him, honoring him. She knew she had witnessed something truly intimate and unique. Hui Yun kept reliving the scene and fell into a meditative state.

The melodies went on flowing, evolving through her psyche; major keys shifting into minor ones with various modalities and tempos. It seemed very unusual, yet the experience was not completely unfamiliar. Hui Yun opened her eyes. There, with his furry and long-whiskered head well above the shimmering waters, ten meters from shore, was Boris, the big-eyed seal!

He looked inquisitively at her, she looked curiously at him. Hui Yun could not be sure, but for a moment it almost appeared as if the animal wished to communicate something, or perhaps, as she later wondered, *had been*. Then Boris seemed to shift his gaze beyond her. Hui Yun turned her head to look around, but she could see no one else, nor detect anything unusual.

CHAPTER 26

Hands Up!

Nanaw caught me in the honey jar... four times. I told her and Jesus I was sorry. *Grace Daisy Rademacher*

The "park police," as Qin Jiang called them, flew out to investigate the "mackie convention" over the lake. The large group was told to disperse and return to their rooms. Jiang was informed that he and his men would have to exit the water. The commander tried to argue that due to the immensity of the caldera, it hardly appeared as if they were in anyone's way.

Ho called out, "Do you know who this man is?"

"Look, I really don't care if he's the Queen of Sheba," the sardonic park attendant replied. Jiang, who rarely endured belittling, simply laughed.

"There is a real risk of a major landslide after this earthquake. A very large movement of earth dislodging could create tremendous waves." The attendant further explained.

"Sounds... exhilarating!" Jiang was thrilled.

"Perhaps for you and your team, but for these people hovering around, it's dangerous. Such waves might rise dozens of meters."

"Understood," sighed Jiang, as he signaled for the Dragons to comply.

The men swam back to their fabulous craft resting quietly on the water and lifted off to return to the rim.

Jiang was exceedingly surprised to spot Hui Yun simply standing, somewhat frozen, at the edge of Wizard Island. He flew in close by, raised the dome visor and called out, "You know, I'm getting rather bored with this place. So, we're heading off to find a better mountain lake to play in. Ah... would you, my dear, like to join us?"

"Umm... umm... sure," was all she could muster.

As she entered the vehicle, Jiang made each of his compatriots sincerely apologize to Hui Yun for their over-the-top prank. At that moment, she found it was not difficult to be genuinely forgiving and nodded her head to them all, reassuringly.

She asked Jiang if they would return to the southern lakeshore area and Pelican Cove. He shook his head, explaining the water there was far too shallow for their planned activities.

The arrival of the Feilong 9 had certainly been beneficial to Jiang in one obvious way. He now had use of the wonderfully sleek, well-equipped, and adequately large transport, the Long Zhua (Dragon Claw), to more fully employ his amusements. The features of the ultramodern craft were beyond extraordinary, with deep underwater and low Earth orbit capabilities.

The stunning, acrylic, Marquise diamond-shaped vehicle touched down on the Rim Village Airpad to await the arrival of Zhao Zhi, who would also join them on their outing.

CHAPTER 27

Habibi

I think… therefore… I happily debate myself all day long. *Zhao Zhi*

The men at Pearlstein's had their fill of drinking beer, ridiculing one another, deep philosophizing and began to retire for the evening. Aaron pushed his chair back slowly as did Jacov.

"I actually don't have my transport tonight because… I crashed it last week. So, walk with me a bit," Jacov said, putting a friendly arm around Aaron. They both headed out the door. "I have a little religious tale you may find amusing. It was years ago when I was a teenager. We were hanging out at the pool and there was some guy visiting from the States. I think he wanted to impress us Sabras, so he blurts out how he hopes America will always support Israel because it was written:

I will bless those who bless you, and curse those who curse you.

"You should have heard me then! I said, 'hey Habibi… dude… are you gonna come here and quote to us from your old Bible, as if you really understood anything about our country?' I practically spit up my lunch and swore at him. You would have laughed yourself silly if you saw his face, he was totally confused. I bet he went home and told his smug, self-righteous Church buddies, 'Oh, my God! Did you know there are these total atheists in Israel, the supposed Land of Faith? Somehow that didn't make it into the brochure.' You're darn right it doesn't make it in!"

Aaron smiled a little, then commented. "Some people still talk about that... when America reversed course and rescinded their support. Shortly after was when they fell into chaos."

"Oh no, are you going superstitious on me? You... you moron! What, you want to believe in curses from the... Bible, of all things? Blessings and curses from an old book? Say it isn't so. I mean, my God, that's so primitive. What do you take me for, an ignoramus?" Jacov was really irritated.

"Well, it did, in fact... actually happen," Aaron stated, trying to be factual.

"I suppose you'll then tell me that the axis of forces which weakened America, and then surrounded Israel, had some kind of judgement rain down on them as well? People want to say it was the Hand of God, but I say it was science, pure and simple. No deities... just... neutrinos... that's what did it. The Israeli scientists gave us ingenious weapons and then... Poof! Our enemies were defeated."

Aaron was somewhat absorbed in his own thoughts, but noticed it was time to separate and continue home down a different street.

"I agree with you, of course," Aaron stated quietly. "I only repeated what others have said."

Jacov, who was feeling quite grandiose, joyously childlike and ever so comfortably drunk, made a courteous, pontifical genuflection and then gave his benediction.

"Good night, my fellow Atheist... I greatly bless you... I prosper you... I... absolve you of all Sin... whatever the heck it is!"

CHAPTER 28

A Lesson Learned

Pets are like little professors. Indeed, my cats have patiently tutored me for years. *Zhao Zhi*

Little Gracie was chasing cute fuzzy chicks around the chicken coop. Several adults watched and chuckled at her antics. The enthusiastic child would get close to catching one, only to have the little birds scatter in all directions.

"O-oh," she cried, and then turned to run and try again. Finally, she was able to corner a small one between the fence and henhouse, and she scooped it up.

"Be careful, young'un, that's just a wee little baby newborn chick," called out Nanaw. "Hold it gently in the holler of yer hand."

Little Gracie looked intently at the small bird she held cupped in her hands. She was simply enchanted.

"I will call you Esther," the child said excitedly.

"Oh, so it's a girl." The small audience laughed.

"Well, I think so." Gracie twirled and swayed her arms from side to side. Ever the flamboyant performer, she danced and sang with enthusiasm for a few minutes.

Little birdie, I'm your friend,
we can play together.
Esther, Esther, Esther,
I'm your bestest, bestest friend.
Esther, Esther, Esther,
I love you, love you, love you so.

Then, suddenly, Gracie's foot caught on a root and she spun to the ground and the tiny bird bounced out of her hand. In a moment, Esther was on her feet and scurried away.

"Young lady, when you hold a baby bird in the holler of yer hand, you best take real good care of it. Yer her protector," Nanaw admonished.

Gracie felt for a little bruise on her knee, which was mostly for show, as she was just simply embarrassed. She took two deliberate breaths and began crying. Sometime later, the girl could be found in her favorite spot in the forest, passionately involved in her most enjoyable pastime, talking with and singing to God.

CHAPTER 29

Cloak-and-Dagger

Gid… eon beat Mid… ian. Hurray!!
Grace Daisy Rademacher

"We call it a Midianite Implosion."

Aaron looked around and spied a tall woman following him, but felt awkward and confused, so he shrugged, turned forward and kept walking.

"It's from the Tanakh," the same voice said. Aaron turned again.

"Are you talking to me? A Midianite what? And… do we know each other?"

"Yes and no," the woman responded quickly. "Don't stop and don't try going home."

"This is crazy, lady, I don't know you and… it's too late for some silly game. Did Jacov put you up to this?"

"No, and I'm trying to help you. You can trust me, I am with special forces. Normally, we invite you to a cordial meeting, but the situation has changed. Please turn right here, down Yefet Street."

"Look, I don't have time for this, so kindly leave me be." Aaron was most annoyed. The sound of sirens erupted in the distance. He paid little attention and kept on walking.

Suddenly, the woman grabbed his arm and said earnestly, "I am Commander Hadasa Mizrahi, find a way to trust me. You cannot go home now, it isn't there anyway."

Through the fog in his brain, Aaron perceived she was trying to warn him about something serious. What it might be, however, was completely bewildering. *The Midianites were some ancient people, what could they possibly have to do with anything? And "Don't go home, it isn't there," what on earth could that mean?*

She squeezed his arm to get his attention once again and spoke intentionally. "Perhaps you can assist us... as you yourself described... sending a robot army into mass confusion... causing them to turn on one another. It's what we refer to as a 'Midianite Implosion' and how the legendary general, Gideon, achieved his great victory over the enemy."

Though Aaron was not completely sure why, he followed her as she turned onto a side street and headed toward a windowless transport. Then he reacted violently.

"Wait, no... not in there. I've watched a lot of movies and you don't get in one of those... *EVER!* How can I trust you? I can't trust you! I'll be unconscious in five seconds or something!" Two security androids approached from the shadows and surrounded Aaron as the gull-wing door opened. They quickly loaded him into the transport and he was unconscious in a mere three-and-a-half seconds. A perfect doppelganger emerged and continued walking down the street.

CHAPTER 30

Through the Acrylic Looking-Glass

For there is nothing hidden that will not be revealed, and nothing concealed that will not be known and illuminated.

Luke 8:17

The Long Zhua soared into the sky. Jiang's communicator picked up a park message informing that all travel beyond the boundaries was strictly prohibited. Yesterday's outing, it would appear, had been thoroughly unauthorized, but the commander was unconcerned. The recording repeated, and Jiang let a specific section play over the cabin speakers.

"...for everyone's safety, interaction with local inhabitants is not permitted. It is also forbidden to introduce or display any modern technology among them as this might generate adverse reactions. Special liaison teams will be deployed shortly to begin culturally sensitive and appropriate contact."

Hui Yun appeared unsettled. Jiang gave her a mildly apologetic look, but in order to lessen her worries and others at the Geopark, he accessed the controls to begin stealth-mode phasing. In a few short moments, the craft and all it carried were completely undetectable to anyone below.

The explorers flew over the vastly forested, mountainous terrain and approached a commanding, snow-covered pyramid-shaped peak. In his ever adventure-loving customary manner, Jiang could not help but try to practically sideswipe the mountain a few times with the Long Zhua. Hui Yun closed her eyes and clung tightly to her armrests, trying to endure the nerve-racking escapade. Zhao Zhi, who was giddy as a school boy, cried out over and over.

"Oooooooooeeeeeeeeee!"

When Jiang had finally tired of the game, he continued toward their destination. Spotting a new lake, Hui Yun could see how truly idyllic the setting was. Log cabins were scattered beneath a rich evergreen canopy along a body of pristine mountain water.

As they approached, the travelers noticed a large meeting of locals on the shoreline of the aptly named Forest Lake. This group's attire appeared similar to the villagers they had previously met yet was not quite as colorful and varied. A lone man stood on a floating platform addressing the crowd. Jiang touched the virtual controls, slowed his descent and digitally amplified the speaker's voice so the party could listen in. Due to the particle dispersion process, the audio was initially jumbled, but after a few moments the sound waves were clarified, enabling them to hear the following announcement.

"... and we have received word from Pelican... they have met some of the outsiders." There were gasps from the crowd. "These newcomers were, it appeared, friendly and non-threatening, which is reassuring. I have taken measures to double our town sentries, so that we will not be caught by surprise. Also... and this is very important, it has been determined we should not divulge any knowledge of the hidden laboratories in the caves."

Now someone in the crowd shouted, "can we be sure the newcomers are peaceful? They've been known to exaggerate a thing or two in Pelican Cove." There was some general laughter. The mayor continued.

"Well, that was, of course, concerning their ongoing 'revival'... and their talk of miracles... and all those angels their little ones said were flying in the sky. This is certainly much different than that. I believe we can trust their impressions."

On the Long Zhua, Jiang waxed devious, "won't this be ever so amusing?"

"No Jiang, you can't... possibly," cried Hui Yun.

"Why not? I'm the Queen of Sheba! Or, who knows, maybe I'm an angel?"

He began the un-phasing process to return the craft to the visible light spectrum. The crowd erupted in no small commotion and pointed in wonder as the futuristic shiny vehicle came into view, hovering above the water. Some ran in fear. The mayor at the podium turned and upon seeing the aircraft, fell backwards.

Jiang raised the dome, looked about, and casually spoke over his broadcast system.

"Hello... everyone."

The assembly on the shore froze in utter shock and amazement. No one blinked. The Feilong members fought hard to suppress their laughter. It was futile. The commander waited a moment and then continued, thoroughly sarcastic, but totally nonchalant.

"I say… but does anyone know of a fine mountain lake we might make use of for the day?"

Jiang silenced his microphone as the military men roared hysterically and wiped tears from their eyes. Although Hui Yun felt terrible for these people, she could not help herself from giggling a little bit either.

The commander lowered his craft further until it hovered ten meters above the water. He gave a signal to his men who now zipped up their wetsuits, fitted small cylinder-shaped packs to their backs and one by one, dove over the side of the Long Zhua. The crowd stood quietly observing.

Jiang walked out onto one of the small wings, as the autopilot landed the craft upon the lake. He raised one hand up high to wave and shouted out to the large, statue-like assembly.

"Have a nice day!" Jiang exclaimed as he dove into the water and joined his comrades.

CHAPTER 31

Quite a Performance

River Otters make me laugh so, cuzz they loves to play!
Grace Daisy Rademacher

"You need to go home now… your shift is over." Arie reminded.

"But what about…"

"I already told you, our beloved Hadasa Mizrahi has gone dark." Arie interrupted Ethan dramatically, while slowly spreading his arms to indicate all their advanced technology was now useless.

"But what does it mean?" Ethan inquired.

"It means… she cannot fully trust Mossad… or even us right now. I imagine she's probably trying to figure out just exactly who is on her tail. Don't worry, she'll make contact when she needs to."

"Are we still monitoring Qin Jiang and his Flying Dragons?" Ethan asked.

"Let's have a look. Beelzebub found them, yes?" Arie touched his virtual console and a timber-lined mountain lake under a beautiful, sunny, cloudless sky appeared on his screen.

"Wow!"

"Lovely!" They were both quite impressed.

"I don't see Qin..." but Arie never got the rest of his sentence out. Quite suddenly and without warning, something shot up rapidly, directly in the center of their virtual screen.

"What the ...?" declared Arie in English. The two sat somewhat dumbfounded, having not seen this particular exercise before. Four more objects surged out of the lake and then it finally became clear what they were seeing.

"Oh my God," Ethan exclaimed, "it's those darn Flying Dragons... flying!"

From the shoreline, Hui Yun, Zhi, and the villagers of Forest Lake beheld the projectiles rocketing up over the water. Jiang had not explained exactly what his planned activities were for the day, but it was now obvious the spectators were in for a treat. The cylinder jet packs could apparently thrust the Feilong from under the water to a great height of about twenty-five meters.

The commandos began demonstrating agile acrobatics as they flew; flips and twists in tuck, pike and layout positions. One emerged performing two dozen rapid somersaults. Next, was a windmill like cart-wheeling routine, and then a comic dive where the individual reclined on his side, with his head propped up on his arm. Hu, the jokester of the bunch, even flew by flailing away on 'air guitar.'

After viewing the first series of over water dives, the crowd quickly became discerning connoisseurs of the unique athletic art form and began whistling and yelling their approval.

Some locals shouted out scores, so that after a masterful-looking effort the lake echoed with roars of "Ten! Ten! Ten!" At one point, a member of the Dragons failed to release his tuck at the right moment and landed his dive flat on his back. Sympathetic "oooh's" resounded from around the shoreline, with Zhi repeating, "oh my, oh my," while one man declared woefully, "zero point five!" However, all of this was merely just a warm up.

There was a pause during which the daring airmen of the lake gathered together in conference. Then, two men emerged flying side by side in unison, performing a series of complicated maneuvers. The new contest appeared to be how perfectly in sync the divers could remain. Eventually, the groups reformed into three sets of three. This was an extremely difficult task for the aerial triplets to achieve complete uniformity, so when perfection was attained, the onlookers were wild with enthusiasm.

Then the men commenced an even more demanding exercise. Here, two flyers emerged opposite one another, angling for a mid-air connection to form a rotating square reminiscent of trapeze artists. It took a number of attempts for the pairs to find their rhythm, but when they had, there was more great excitement from the lakeshore. This was also just a beginning point.

The next forty-five minutes were spent with the men working toward a new level of synchronization. The goal was to form the mid-air rotating square and simultaneously launch an individual flyer through its center. This was clearly no small challenge. First, the two had to create the shape, and then the third man had to be correctly angled (at ninety degrees) and perfectly timed to "thread the needle."

There were some mid-air collisions and "almost had it" moments. Yet, it was almost more enjoyable to see the attempts when the timing or the angling was terribly off, and no one was anywhere near anyone else. The men laughed or pointed fingers of blame at each other. In the end, the feat was achieved flawlessly, twice. It truly made for quite a grand finale. The residents erupted in exuberant praise, and far away even two otherwise sober-looking Israeli operatives also cheered. Jiang was apparently satisfied with the efforts of his training exercise, and the Dragons began a playful and leisurely swim to shore.

Unlike the other day, the inhabitants of this village appeared reluctant to interact with the visitors. Many of them had remained viewing the Feilong training session, while others returned to various chores and activities. Hui Yun had only spoken with a few individuals during the day. The mayor of Forest Lake, Sam Cartwright, had been friendly with Hui Yun and Zhi, but had left after a time. Hui Yun wandered about studying the pretty village cabins for a while, then returned to the lake and found Sam and Zhi now fishing from the shore while scrutinizing the diving routines. She overheard the mayor speaking.

"I used to be a pilot…" Sam said.

"Ten years commercial service… and my father was a pilot… and so was his father. Yeah, really, my grandfather flew fighter jets in Korea. Then he came back and was eventually promoted to the space program. He worked with John Glenn, the first American in space. Ha… and now look at us… we Americans… ever so humbled." The mayor grew pensive.

"By the rivers of Babylon, there we sat down and wept," he said despondently.

Hui Yun did not understand what this meant.

She then observed as Sam walked right up to the pointed nose of the Long Zhua, which extended over the pebbled beach, and for some inexplicable reason, he punched it. The others watched in disbelief.

Sam stood there amazed as he realized that the translucent shell of the ultra-modern vehicle had given slightly to the force of his blow. The material was malleable, to better absorb the impact of shrapnel and weaponry. *Ingenious,* he thought. He studied it in close detail, marveling at its design.

"What is… ah… 'Mondo Twinkie Find?'" Hui Yun blurted out her question to not only help change the mood of the conversation, but also because she had been curious.

"What, oh," Sam laughed. "That's a humorous tale, I guess. Way back, we really did find Twinkies every so often. You know, those yummy cream-filled sponge cakes. Now, I think it has more to do with finding any quality stash from long ago. Mainly preserved foods… freeze dried is always best… or a big find of anything, really. So, a 'Twinkie Find' is something very special."

"Oh, I see." Hui Yun smiled at him.

"You know, before the Humbling, we used to put up lots of rations and supplies in bunkers and buried containers. Occasionally, we still come across these."

Jiang and his team now emerged, sauntering from the shallows onto the shoreline.

"Amazing!" Hui Yun yelled.

The commander gave her a nod. The men pulled down the tops of their wet suits to catch the warm mountain sun on their undoubtedly cold bodies, having just spent several hours in the lake. This revealed some fantastically muscled torsos and arms, providing an exceptional opportunity for Hui Yun to casually study the elite group's flying dragon tattoos.

"I'm glad you enjoyed the exercise," Jiang began. "Of course, we are not performers. We are learning to work as one, to become intuitive and seamless as a unit. To see if we can know what each other is thinking... and, I mean, in an instant." Jiang looked around, then back out over the lake at something almost unseen.

Eleven thousand kilometers away, two somewhat sleepy Israeli operatives sat transfixed, still observing the image. The camera zoomed in precisely on Jiang, and as he looked up right in their direction, Arie and Ethan quickly sat back in their chairs. Jiang now spoke as if on stage, dramatic and playful.

"We are not at all to be confused with some order of celebrated performers. No, oh no... we are but simple... military men, mere soldiers, and of no account. Yet, of tangible worth because of who it is we serve... the grandest and oldest of our planet's empires, the Great Dragon. And, our very lives, and perhaps China's future may one day depend on the training we do here today!"

"Bravo! Bravo!" Zhi clapped. "Why, you should have done Shakespeare."

Jiang knelt down and reached into an equipment bag. He stood up with a shiny, hand-held weapon which he immediately fired over the lake. The smart bullet found its mark, there was a small explosion with a puff of smoke, and far away two Israelis sat studying a virtual screen of pure static.

Zhi was mortified by the shooting and stood speechless. The military man ignored the elderly professor's expression and remarked charmingly, "I thought you'd like that little speech. I hammed it up, just for you."

Jiang now addressed the Forest Lake mayor.

"We are already aware of the underground labs in your lava caves. It is those you know nothing about which concern us most."

Hui Yun was very surprised to learn such information and would have inquired to understand more, but a loud noise interrupted the conversation.

"Eeee-ya-hi!" It was the last member of the team emerging from the lake, triumphantly. He held up a net containing a dozen or more large, fine-looking rainbow trout. "Dinner is served!" the underwater fisherman exclaimed.

"See that, Zhi? You don't have to wait all day and try to catch your entrée, we've spared you the trouble... compliments of the Flying Dragons!" Qin Jiang spoke with a playful, yet arrogant bravado.

Not one to ever seemed rattled, except by his own internal regrets, Zhi replied casually, but firmly, "you never seem to grasp the deeper significance, do you, my friend? Going fishing isn't about the mere catching of fish. No, it is much, much more... it is about entering into stillness and contemplation."

CHAPTER 32

Where Am I?

On the outskirts of Tel Aviv in an undisclosed location

> *Confusion... a simply awful state of mind... not unlike the time, many years ago, when I tried to drive my way around Newark, New Jersey.* *Zhao Zhi*

"Wait until he learns you plan to smuggle him into America... of all places," an unknown voice remarked. Aaron blinked and slightly shook his numb-feeling head. He was no longer on the street, but where he was exactly, he had no idea. Feeling tingly and delirious, he decided to lie still and listen.

"Now, let's not get ahead of ourselves," Commander Hadasa Mizrahi said quietly, "it is just a rumor. We have no solid, irrefutable intelligence, yet."

Aaron's mind swirled. Although he strained to focus on the conversation, he was still too groggy to concentrate fully. Over the next few minutes he heard several scattered phrases which caught his attention, but he was never completely sure if it had simply been a dream.

"Perhaps a… human-android hybrid…"

"…a genuine super-soldier?"

"Yes, it violates dozens of treaties..."

"The ultimate weapon…"

"… we are now both locked in a race to discover…"

Then Aaron drifted off completely and everything faded to black.

A hologram broadcast in the center of the room. It was breaking news coverage of a fire raging on a city block.

"What is that?" Aaron blurted out as he returned to consciousness.

Hadasa gave a look to Simon who put down his drink and hit some controls to terminate the projection.

"That is, I believe, the street where you live," Hadasa stated plainly.

"What! What on earth is going on?" Aaron would have stood up, but he was still too dizzy.

"Well, basically, somebody wants what you have," she informed.

"I don't have… or know anything. I don't have a clue what this is all about." Aaron put his arm to his forehead, extremely overcome with stress. Hadasa moved closer and stroked his face with one hand and held up his wrist with her other.

"This has got to go," she told him. "When you calm down, I need you to shave off your beard and I'll alter your biometrics… to keep our trail dark. Not exactly sure who we can trust, yet."

"Wait a minute, you're going to kidnap me, and… and drug me and God knows what else and now we're supposed to get chummy and… and chop off my nice long beard? I don't think so." Aaron folded his arms in a huff.

"It may be hard to believe, but we probably saved your life."

Aaron was quiet for a time, lost in thought, then he responded, "well, you might have been a little nicer about it!"

"If I couldn't have gotten you into the transport, I would likely have shot you," was Hadasa's firm response.

"Oh, wow, I see. Well lady, if that's what you're into, between you and me, I do not want to go out on a date with you any time soon… I can tell you that. Now why on earth am I here?""

"Apparently, you had some discussion at the bar tonight."

"Wait, how did you… know?" and he paused for a few moments. "What? About robots? It was all just… talk." Aaron was baffled.

"No, about deceiving robots, tricking them… getting them to sin," she corrected nicely.

"That's what this is about? Oh, I see… ah… so did the bots and droids from around the world suddenly get all paranoid and… and have come to try and kill me?!" Aaron quipped.

"We're not ruling anything out, just yet."

"Sounds to me like they need some major group therapy or something." The computer wizard was beginning to see this was no time for humor. He took a deep breath and spoke frankly.

"It was only just a prank. I like pranks, you know, and I… I've developed ways to trick advanced systems."

"And…?" Hadasa looked intently at Aaron.

"Well… I shut down the security at the Central Bank the other day."

"My God… there's mountains of shekels and priceless art in those vaults," gasped Simon. "People keep their gold and diamonds in there… unbelievable!"

"Yeah, it's the fifth bank I've done it to," Aaron said softly.

Simon spit out an entire mouthful of soda and cried, "how on earth did you do it?"

"Did you ever take anything?" inquired Hadasa.

"Steal? No… of course not, I just do it for the adrenaline rush," Aaron replied. "They never go public, bad for business… so… I thought no one knew."

"This may possibly be worse than I imagined," said a pensive-looking Hadasa.

"So, how did you pull it off?" asked Simon, on the edge of his seat.

"Hey, what does she mean? Okay… well, I bypassed most of their defenses using an emergency repair protocol for a leaky sewer pipe… and then, you know, you drop a few stench simulators, and everybody runs."

"That's it? That's your big techno-ploy, you get in as the plumber?" Simon was astounded.

"Well, that's how I did it last time," Aaron remarked with a slightly devious smile.

"See, I told you I like the way he thinks," Hadasa said to Simon.

"Yeah, but there are security droids all over, they aren't going to run," Simon observed.

"Not a problem. Beforehand, you casually schmooze with security... you know… sweet talk them!"

Simon looked very puzzled and Aaron, finally feeling energized, waxed poetic.

"The heartbeat of all androids is an algorithm. Their digital daydreams are the envy of a Physics Nobel Laureate. Therefore… what on earth do you do? Well, it's patently obvious. Engage those artificial minds in some light conversation on dark matter or quantum gravity, Schrödinger's cat, or maybe the ever elusive… Unified Field Theory. Those are topics that are simply yummy sweet brain-candy for their neurons. And so then, believe me… you'll have made some friends for life!

"Now, what does 'worse' mean, exactly?" Aaron said turning wide-eyed toward Hadasa, who then bluntly answered his question.

"Mafia."

"Mafia?"

"Mafia. We could be dealing with nothing more than your friendly… neighborhood… Israeli… Mafia."

"What?" Aaron buried his head. "I sure do wish I could believe in Someone or Something Beyond… or just about anything right now!"

CHAPTER 33

Pressing In

. . . your bestest friend ever!
Grace Daisy Rademacher

Hui Yun reflected on another memorable day. The Feilong 9 made a fire by the lake, cooked the trout and spent the afternoon laughing heartily at a number of inside jokes. Occasionally, some of the men engaged in small competitions on the lakeshore, doing hand stand push-ups or wrestling in the shallows. She marveled at all their endless, extraordinary energy.

Jiang then dropped Hui Yun back at the hotel in the early evening and said that he and his men would be busy for a time. With a free night to spend as she wished, she knew exactly what to do.

Hui Yun brought up her holographic screen and touched some virtual keys. An index appeared of the Yongheng Dehua (Eternal Words), the collected writings of great master teachers. Hui Yun had only been a casual follower of her religion during most of her life. Now, she found herself filled with an inner longing for more of this curious hint of God's presence she felt drawing her.

Twenty years ago, China experienced a spiritual awaking of its own. She was just a mere girl of eleven and had not really understood at the time all that was occurring. There had been a great tumult in the streets of her country once again, even violent protests, such as the car bombing, which had taken her father and emotionally scarred Hui Yun over these many years.

Then came the 'Enlightenment,' or Qishi, which was a decisive moment in the country's history. During this time, in a thoroughly unexpected move, the government itself spearheaded a social campaign which openly embraced and encouraged religious faith. There was an official unifying of several great spiritual traditions and all of China was, in a sense, "Enlightened" into this newly formed *Church of Edification*.

The Yongheng Dehua, or Eternal Words, was the foundation and codex of the movement. It contained various teachings from the Buddha, Confucius, Laozi, the Christ and some lesser known divines. She had always found the quotations of Confucius to be the most interesting. In her childhood, Hui Yun's father had often encouraged her with the adage from the wise sage about learning to rise every time you fall.

Now Hui Yun sought to understand much more about this Jesus of the Bible she had recently heard so much about. She touched the screen to access his teachings.

Do unto others as you would have them do unto you, was projected in front of her.

This was certainly well known. The Golden Rule, it was called. The Parable of the Sower was next to be displayed. *Behold, the sower went out to sow…*

Then she read how Jesus had said, *If your eye be single, your whole body will be filled with light*. One of the villagers quoted this the other day. What on earth did this curious phrase mean exactly? She touched the commentary key and a virtual lecturer appeared explaining "the progressive stages of enlightenment," however, she quickly lost interest.

Hui Yun was compelled to walk on her balcony. She tried speaking with God a little but felt somewhat silly and insincere. Then, sitting back in a chair, she thought upon the words, if your eye be single. She was determined to connect with this rather indescribable *Presence* that was stirring inside her. *Jesus, I want to focus only on you. I want my eye to be single upon you. I want and need you to fill me with light.*

At first, she was merely involved in an exercise, but then, ever so slightly she began to experience something within her spirit. It was gentle like a breeze and quenching to an inner thirst she had always known but had never understood. It was a cool liquid spilling upon the desert floor. *Was this what was meant by "knowing God,"* Hui Yun wondered? She pressed in deeper and further into the encounter.

O Lord, reveal yourself to me. Fill me with this life-giving Spirit. Quench my inner thirst, I just want more and more and more of you!

CHAPTER 34

Run!

Action movies are most certainly financed by the Popcorn Barons.

Zhao Zhi

Hadasa endeavored to explain to Aaron why he had been under minimal government surveillance. With his unique skill set and overall techno-savvy, such an individual could help to decipher encrypted communications or even thwart an overwhelming robot invasion, as he had boasted of doing.

Aaron protested, saying he was not truly military minded, just a computer geek who enjoyed gaming. Although, he did have to admit the idea of defeating advanced AI through subterfuge was akin to scaling the "Techie Mount Everest."

"Deceiving a robotic force could be like unleashing a Frankenstein… or a Golem!" Simon said excitedly.

"Ha! Ha! Right you are, friend," returned Aaron enthusiastically. "And once the monster has been loosed, anything can happen. They might even turn against their Maker!"

Hadasa sought to quiet Aaron down and reminded him that someone else had been observing him, as well. The happy grin left his face.

Simon heard the cat scratching at the back door and asked if he could let the animal in. Hadasa hesitated at first, then nodded consent. Her gaze followed him as he rounded a partition. She was just about to remark to Aaron they could not remain hiding in the slums much longer, when the door opened, the cat hissed, and there was a momentary commotion.

Simon returned holding his neck and fell to his knees, frothing at the mouth. His eyes were fully rolled back in his head as he keeled over, face first. Hadasa jumped and spun toward the front of the house. Lying low, she grabbed something off her belt, pushed the door open and tossed the device with a powerful side arm thrust. Instantly, a great brilliance lit up outside and did not diminish.

"It's the Mob! It's the Mob! It's the..." Aaron screamed.

"Shut up!" Hadasa shouted as she practically flew back to Aaron, grabbed him by the shirt and led him up the stairs to the flat roof. As they emerged, she threw another blinder in the air.

"Close your eyes!" she yelled, "and *RUN!*" She twisted his body to the left and they raced as fast as they could, leaping from rooftop to rooftop. Hadasa again grabbed at her belt and launched a small object straight up. Aaron expected to see the same blinding light as before, but nothing happened. They kept on running, two more houses, four more, and as they crossed to the next, a gunman suddenly emerged on the roof, holding a very modern and lethal-looking weapon in his arms.

"How about we take a little breather?" the man suggested.

Hadasa and Aaron stopped dead in their tracks and raised their arms. Aaron might have responded to the inquiry with a, *sounds like a good idea,* or something to that effect, but he was way too winded to have gotten out a word.

"Now, down on your faces, quickly!"

Aaron was only too happy to comply and lowered to his knees. Hadasa hesitated, looked directly at the adversary and made a very slight nod with her head. In an instant, the gunman fell forward as the back of his cranium was hit hard by the microguard, commonly called the stone of David, which she had deployed a minute earlier.

"Move," Hadasa ordered Aaron. "Don't stop till I tell you."

They crossed over a half dozen more structures, descended the stairs and burst onto an alleyway, shifting from the area of close-lying, flat-roofed houses to a blighted industrial region of the city. Hadasa spotted an abandoned warehouse and led Aaron inside.

"You're going to stay put here. I'll arrange transport. Can't use my communicator, too risky." She shot a look toward several high stacks of pallets and said, "hide yourself in there and remain out of sight. I should be back in a few hours."

She went to the entranceway, looked carefully into the alley and disappeared.

Aaron hid and assessed his situation, shaking uncontrollably and sweating profusely. *Oh, damn, you are so screwed!* He had no real idea of what to do and certainly, what might come next. The last actual praying he had done was years ago at his Bar Mitzvah. Finally, he thought, *Well, what the heck*. So, he began to sing, softly but with some actual sincerity,

"Barukh ata Adonai Elohainu melekh ha'olam…"

CHAPTER 35

Gotcha!

They shall mount up with wings, as eagles. *The Prophet Isaiah*

The Chinese squadron rose swiftly into the sky and surrounded the lone Israeli Alenia Aermacchi fighter jet. The Star of David shot precipitously beneath them, rolling in a death spiral, correcting just before impact. The Israeli plane then disappeared into the canyon maze of the Arabah. The Chinese jet formation doubled back hard, fanning out in hot pursuit.

Nine Cats and a Mouse! was heard over the com.

The People's Liberation Air Force pilots dove into the ravines of the most desolate real estate on earth. The rugged cliffs, gulches and valleys seemed to contain virtually no life whatsoever. The craggy rock and stone terrain was so otherworldly, one might just as likely be scraping across the surface of Mars.

The rolling jet fighter planes deftly traversed the winding gorges. These were the absolute best trained pilots in the world. Years of preparation, a communal Spartan existence, and daily combat exercises made them practically born and bred killing machines. A brainwave guidance system in the Chinese jets allowed for optimum control and instantaneous maneuvering. The synchronization of these men with their crafts was a highly-choreographed performance.

"Have visual on 'Bluestar.'" (The generic nickname for all Israeli Defense Forces hardware.)

The Israeli jet emerged from the rocky hills, blazing like a comet, heading due south with three jets close on its heels.

"Fire at will."

The Chinese attack birds launched hypersonic missiles which closed in rapidly on the target. An instant before contact, the "Bluestar" made an extraordinary and difficult hard left around the mountain of Masada. The missiles veered to follow, but could not mimic the maneuver, and a fireball rose one hundred meters into the sky as they careened into the cliffside. The Chinese planes slowed slightly to better round the mountain fortress. As they did, three air mines the Israeli pilot had left hidden by the rocks deployed and within milliseconds there occurred some rather spectacular aircraft destruction, in triplicate.

The Bluestar shot like a bullet toward the southern end of the Dead Sea, very low, a mere three meters above the surface. Enemy fire was already raining down. The Israeli released a torpedo then veered off high to the northwest, all the while returning fire and spinning evasively to avoid numerous missiles. She commenced another impossible-looking screaming aerial descent. At the final instant, the jet pulled up and began flying fast and low, heading due south over the salty sea.

Two Chinese jets had undertaken a similar tactic and were heading north, just above the glistening surface.

All planes were firing laser cannons and smart missiles freely, which were mostly deflected by the particle shielding. For any missiles that slipped through, the planes spun acrobatically to avoid them. The jets were on a clear collision course, only moments from direct contact.

The Israeli pilot saw an oval appear in her visor. Her pupil moved quickly up and down. In an instant, an enormous underwater explosion occurred, creating a fountain fifty meters high with a fireball twice as large. The Chinese attack birds were engulfed in the melee. As they emerged, the Bluestar fired only twice, easily finishing off the greatly damaged planes, and two flaming wrecks plowed into the sea. The Israeli fighter plane continued south unopposed, toward the Negev.

"You complete imbeciles!" yelled Qin Jiang, utterly disgusted, terminating the virtual program. He let loose a tirade of obscenities the likes of which had seldom been heard and finished with, "oh you stupid, worthless Feilong pretenders!" Jiang was beside himself.

The members of the military unit exchanged glances with one another, not speaking. Hu opened his mouth to say something, but Jiang stopped him.

"Don't try to tell me those are not actual maneuvers. We have observed their very best pilot performing them. She is truly one with her bird and actually has cornered that ravine at those very speeds."

The Flying Dragons were incredulous.

"Indeed… she is a Tiger… and I cannot wait until I face her myself!"

CHAPTER 36

Night Ride

Joy makes my unhappies go bye-bye!
Grace Daisy Rademacher

Flying, Little Gracie was flying way up high in the sky. She was above the clouds now, which were so very light and fluffy beneath her. She reached down and scooped up a tiny wisp in her hand and tried to lick it, but it merely got her face wet.

Gracie rolled onto her back and mimicked swimming upon the cloud. A look of delight was on her face. *This is better than cookies and ice cream with huckleberries!* she thought.

Birds appeared from several directions and joined her. They were of different varieties, shapes and sizes, many of which Gracie recognized and some she did not. The brightly colored birds were now flocking in vast numbers and flew along with her toward the sun. It was an extraordinary throng, a sea of flapping wings.

On the horizon a dark cloud appeared. Lightning flashed and then the delayed thunder rumbled through after several seconds. Vicious looking ravens and vultures approached in great numbers from the opposite direction. They arrived very swiftly and began scrapping with the other birds. Feathers flew and many of the creatures began to fall from the sky.

Two large, protective eagles soared to defend Gracie. Yet, before they could reach her a menacing raven plunged at the girl. She recoiled in terror and began to fall through the cloud. Tremendous panic set in as she spun and whirled, descending rapidly to the earth.

Gracie saw one more billow below her with wisps of white fluff that looked like upturned fingers. By the means of some unseen force, she was caught and held suspended in the palm of the hand-shaped cloud.

A glimmering angel with very large wings, a wildly fluttering robe and shiny trinkets in his hair flew in close beside Gracie. He placed a great ram's horn to his lips and gave a mighty blast. Then the angel made a powerful declaration which echoed across the sky.

"Jubilee!"

Gracie suddenly awoke and repeated the word, though she did not know its meaning.

DAY 4

Chapter 37

Musings

Imagination; the land where an inner harvest of possibilities and impossibilities blossom plentifully together.

Zhao Zhi

Hui Yun literally awoke with a smile, sensing an inner peace she could not understand. She thought upon her intriguing adventures of the last few days; entering an undiscovered world, learning more about God, communicating with a seal. Suddenly, as she contemplated these experiences, a bewildering wave of doubt washed over her. *It appeared to be a legitimate question to ask, was she even mentally stable?*

Now, Hui Yun felt the tangible weight of fear begin to literally pin her down. Her initially calm mind was beset with worry and distress, and she was not at all sure of what to do. Finally, she determined to try and rise and follow her usual course of morning exercise.

Hui Yun brought up her fitness file and searched the virtual key for a scene that might strike her interest.

Holodance, also known as Hollydance, was enormously popular across much of Asia and had been for the better part of a decade. Famous clips from Hollywood's golden film era were projected in virtual reality, allowing participants to join the scene.

This morning Hui Yun thought she might "take a spin" with the always debonair Fred Astaire. She felt a bit intimidated and smiled shyly as the hologram performer held out his hand to hers. At first, it was hard to move her legs, but she forced herself, and endeavored to mimic the smoothness and style of the master dancer's display of effortless grace. In the end, she experienced quite a workout.

Zhi, in his room, stood inside a holographic console surrounded by the compelling sights and exuberant sounds of an orchestra and choir in an ornate and historic concert hall. The professor was rapturously employed at his virtual post, enthusiastically conducting Mahler's Eighth Symphony, the "Symphony of a Thousand." He furiously worked his baton and arms in the customary patterns to control the enormous choir and orchestra's tempo and dynamics. When appropriate, Zhi would cast a powerful glance toward each of the soloists to cue them for their many captivating parts. He was thoroughly engrossed in the marvels of Mahler.

After the piece concluded, he thought for a bit, then requested some archival footage to play in his holodome. The image changed to that of a solitary individual standing bravely in front of an approaching column of army tanks. The daring exploit was extraordinary, riveting, and ever so stirring. The numerous intimidating tanks were brought to a halt as the lone man used his own defenseless body to block their progress. Great tears welled up in Zhi's eyes as he was fully overcome with emotion. The distinguished elder statesman of the great nation of China fell to his knees and wept.

CHAPTER 38

Anthem of the Heart

When I sings a song to Jesus... he smiles.
Grace Daisy Rademacher

Malachi wandered towards the woods to find himself a solitary place to think and pray. He shared the growing concerns of his community about the tremendous activity now being spotted to the north. Two years ago, work had begun on the Crater Lake redesign, but it had remained strictly off limits. With no contact between Pelican Cove and the newcomers, the impact on the village had been minimal. Today, however, as a number of enormous airships hovered in the sky and landed in the Geopark, the telling signs could not be ignored any longer.

Major change, for good or for ill, was imminent.

The stoic teenager found himself unusually troubled and filled with questions. His mind was caught up for a time in confusion, until he heard a cheerful young voice singing among the trees. Malachi walked past some bushes into a small glen and found Gracie Rademacher there with a beaming smile upon her face.

"So, Little Gracie, what are you doing today?" the teenager inquired.

"Hi, Malachi. I'm singing to God."

"That's wonderful, can I listen for a time?"

"Sure. I... I had this dream where I could fly like a birdie, but nasty ravens came at me and so, I fell… and… and then this great big hand made of fluffy cloud caught hold of me and kept me safe!"

"Wow!" Malachi remarked.

Gracie held out an arm in front of her, cupped her hand and signaled to him to do the same. Then she began to sing. The child's voice was pure and honest and captivating.

I'm in the holler of yer hand
I'm in the holler of yer hand
I'm in the holler of yer hand
O God I loves you!

As she repeated the simple lines, she bobbed her hand up and down, so he could understand how he was being held, too. Malachi was deeply touched and wiped away a few tears that had collected on his cheeks.

"There was also this great big angel in my dream who flew up and said real loud, 'Jubilee!' What does it mean, Malachi, what does it mean?" the curious girl inquired.

He nodded with elation and remarked, "wow, oh wow! That's the Day of Good News… the time to proclaim freedom throughout the land!" Then, after a moment, he spoke gently, "Gracie, most people will better understand if you sing '*hollow* of *your* hand.' But it is very, very special." Malachi now appeared somewhat introspective again and slowly walked off into the woods.

CHAPTER 39

Letters from an Inner Bard

How sweet are your words to my taste,
sweeter than honey to my mouth!
Psalm 119:103

Although the previous night had been a significant time of internal breakthrough, Hui Yun now found herself cloaked beneath an inexplicable heaviness. The roller coaster ride of the last few days had been run on adrenaline, and her emotional tank was thoroughly empty. After exercising, she had prayed and read one of the parables of Jesus, yet her efforts left her restless and dissatisfied.

Hui Yun recalled that Remedy, the friendly teenage girl in Pelican Cove, had mentioned something about passages of the Psalms being "medicine for one's heart." Hui Yun searched her virtual library to locate the collection of spiritual songs which was only vaguely familiar to her.

"The Lord cares about our 'ups and downs.'" Remedy explained and then declared a most curious notion about God.

"You keep track of all my sorrows. You have collected all my tears in your bottle."

Hui Yun marveled at the thought.

The Book of Psalms now appeared on her virtual screen along with an index of sub-categories, enabling her to sample different themes and topics. Hui Yun read slowly and thoughtfully for quite some time. She found candid expressions of joy and despair, brokenness and rejoicing, which seemed to address the entire spectrum of human emotion.

Under the heading of *Discouragement,* Hui Yun recognized a verse Mayor Sam had spoken the other day.

By the rivers of Babylon,
There we sat down and wept,
When we remembered Zion.
Upon the willows…
We hung up our harps.

Hui Yun pictured how these ancient people mourned after being carried into exile. It startled her to realize they had gone through a great Humbling, and she now understood why these Bible-believing Americans saw God's hand in their own national crisis. Later, she read how the Jewish people were overcome with euphoria after they returned to their land.

When the LORD restored the fortunes of Zion,
we were like those who dream.
Then our mouth was filled with laughter,
and our tongue with shouts of joy;
then they said among the nations,
"The LORD has done great things for them."

As she perused more of the text, Hui Yun found a verse which accurately captured her own internal feelings.

Why are you in despair, O my soul?
And why have you become disturbed within me?
Hope in God for I shall again praise Him
For the help of His presence

She took some comfort in the exhortation. Then, the touching imagery of one particular Psalm caught her attention and challenged her thinking. Hui Yun had always believed that God was transcendent, distant and unconcerned, but this rich passage showed otherwise. God was also personal and exceedingly close.

O Lord, you have searched me and known me…
You understand my thought from afar…
And are intimately acquainted with all my ways…
For You formed my inward parts;
You wove me in my mother's womb.
I will give thanks to You, for
I am fearfully and wonderfully made…
And in Your book were all written
The days that were ordained for me,
When as yet there was not one of them

Finally, she came across the most compelling phrase of her entire study.

Deep calls to deep at the sound of Your waterfalls;
All Your breakers and Your waves have rolled over me.

Hui Yun pondered the meaning of this for quite some time. For her, plunging to the depths of Crater Lake had been a similar, overwhelming, internal experience.

CHAPTER 40

Lost at Sea!

Courage! Courage! I have admired the brave all my life... generally from afar.
Zhao Zhi

As Aaron surveyed the vast horizon, light swells gently rocked his small boat from side to side. It all seemed pleasant enough with a bright sunny sky, but he had absolutely no idea where he was or which direction he should go. From high above he was no more than a tiny speck in a great ocean. No wonder he felt so lost and alone. Then clouds gathered to his north, and the wind and waves grew in intensity.

The sky darkened considerably, and the sea spray began whipping wildly, biting into Aaron's face. He flailed with his oars but could make no progress. The storm was now a driving tempest, with sheets of rain and incredibly powerful breakers. Another boat pushed by these forces suddenly drew close to Aaron's. In it, an old bearded man was yelling.

"I say, but do you have any light with you?"

Unexpectedly, a piercing noise now arose which could be heard above the wild squall. Aaron shouted to the man.

"What is it?"

The sailor gave him an earnest look and cried,

"Sea Dragon! Behold... the Dragon cometh!"

The unearthly tumult grew deafening and Aaron was overcome with terror at the enormous disturbance in the waters. Emerging powerfully from the sea, with fiery illumination in its eyes, nose and mouth, was the head of a behemoth, fantastical dragon. After a few moments, it became apparent that it was an extraordinary craft, a vehicle whose midsection went on for dozens of meters.

Through large windows Aaron could make out legions of identical-looking, black-haired men in white outfits, seated in rows. In the final window appeared a Queen on a throne wearing a crystal crown. For a brief instant the regal woman turned, looked directly at the helpless boaters and laughed. Then the whip-like tail section emerged from the sea, thrashing furiously, and swung toward Aaron. He was forced to quickly dive into the waves just as his little boat was smashed to bits. He held on fiercely to some shattered timber to stay afloat.

After some time, the storm finally passed, the sky lightened, and Aaron was surrounded by very different waters, lovely and clear. Tall waves rolled through at long intervals but were not so difficult to manage. Due to the clarity of the water, he could see directly through an approaching swell. He studied this for some time, then realized his predicament was still utterly hopeless. But then, shouts arose around him.

"Ahoy!" and "here, over here!" could now be heard coming from many sailors who had apparently suffered a similar fate.

Through the prism of a wave he beheld an inspiring sight, a great vessel was fast approaching. Sturdy and elegant, with its many sails billowing, an impressive nineteenth-century clipper ship rose and fell as it cut its way across the shimmering crystal sea. Aaron cried out in desperate hope that he would be seen by the crew.

"Help me! Here, I'm over here!"

Others were lifted to safety as a rising wave took them to the side rail. His adrenaline was pumping. If the timing was right, he might be delivered.

Sails full, the boat loomed larger. Aaron felt he might only get one chance. A wave rose beneath him and carried him high, just as the ship was passing. He was close. A man stood leaning over the rail, arms outstretched. Their hands almost met, and Aaron looked in amazement at the noble and compassionate face of his would-be benefactor. It was the Captain of the ship himself, reaching down for the rescue.

Suddenly a rat scrambled over Aaron's shoes, jolting him awake. After a brief moment, he became cognizant of some rather cold, harsh realities. He was in an abandoned warehouse in Tel Aviv and hunted by unknown, ruthless assassins. He felt his shirt and found it was all wet from having drooled on himself. *No wonder I dreamt I was lost at sea,* he thought.

Looking around at his bleak surroundings, a tangible darkness closed in. It was the most despairing, lonely moment in Aaron's entire life. He had no idea what his fate would be, as Commander Hadasa Mizrahi was nowhere to be found.

CHAPTER 41

Inner Journeys

Look in eyes
Eyes look back

Boris, a Nerpa

To glide, to swim, to be free from all constraints, to soar; Hui Yun was immersed in the ever-stunning grandeur of Crater Lake. The marvelous azure and cobalt world surrounding her was pierced by golden light shafts extending deep into the expanse. She was being propelled through the liquid domain by an unseen force, making no effort at all to swim. Beside her was Boris, the ever-playful seal. He rolled from side to side and watched her with his large coal-black eyes. Together, the two of them were moving swiftly, as if on their way toward something or someplace important.

Soon they were joined by other fascinating creatures; swordfish, dolphins and large whales, all traveling in the same direction. Looking at them closely, Hui Yun sensed they possessed unusual intelligence. It was a tremendous host; an aquatic army of sorts.

Gazing up into the sky, Hui Yun then saw a great flock of pelicans descending. Plunging into the crystal-clear waters, the birds momentarily appeared to resemble something more akin to angels. They dove into the unfathomable depths and then ascended, launching back into the sky. The entire scene was a marvelous display of coordinated animal athleticism and the beautiful dance of nature. Hui Yun was totally enthralled.

Suddenly, loud vocalizations were heard as the troop communicated with one another. For an instant, the human member of the group gained the ability to interpret the strange language, which seemed to be verses of a very odd, haunting song.

From ancient times await we all,
The Day undoing Earth's undoing.
To Myst'ry ever shall we call,
Hope lies within the Great Renewing.

Hui Yun listened with wonder but could make no sense of the riddle.

Eventually, some of the creatures began to drop out of the entourage. Then more and more swam off, until only Boris and Hui Yun were left. They glided into a cove and up to the shoreline. Hui Yun's parents stood there, awaiting her arrival. She looked up at them quite surprised and cried out.

"Look, Daddy, look, Mommy, I can swim with the seals!"

Hui Yun reached out to touch them, but then awoke, falling forward in her chair. She had apparently drifted during her scripture meditation into a deep sleep.

The vividness and frequency of her dreams of late had become almost too much to handle, straining her emotions. Hui Yun had lost her father twenty years ago. To see him appear so real and alive was thoroughly inexplicable and overwhelming. She realized that not only was Zhao Zhi having a difficult anniversary, so too was she.

Hui Yun wept.

"Help Lord, I'm afraid I might overflow your bottle."

CHAPTER 42

Brush Arbor Revival

You can love him or pester him... but I know Jesus smiles because you's askin'.
Grace Daisy Rademacher

Having risen after a noontime nap, Little Gracie played in her lean-to. She placed a number of hand-made dolls and sock monkeys in sitting positions and sang them one of her homespun ditties she had written with her friend Malachi.

He couldn't move, he was asleep
Don't make a sound, don't make a peep
But then he wiggled all his toes
And he rose!
Yes, he rose!

The light was gone, the night was here
But soon the dawn was coming near
A seed falls to the ground and grows
Yes, he rose
He rose

You love me, and I love you
Impossible is what you do

I love you and you love me
You went to sleep
Day one, two, three
And then you wiggled all your toes
And you rose!
Yes, you rose!
A seed falls to the ground and grows
Yes, you rose!
You rose!

Gracie held up a doll whose side was torn open, revealing the fluffy sheep's wool stuffing within. She engaged the captive audience with her emerald green eyes and spoke passionately.

"The Lord Jesus said, 'Come to Me, all who are weary and burdened, and I will give you rest.' Becuzz of bad things we all do, we get boo-boos in our hearts," Gracie said as she pulled the fabric on the doll's body to cover the opening. "But the good news is… they put these big needles in Jesus' hands and with them he can stitch up all our wounds." She looked intently at her "congregation" and pressed home her pitch. "So, don't you want Jesus to be your bestest friend in the whole world… right now?"

"I do, I do!" two-and-a-half-year-old Martha shouted from her bed. Gracie had not noticed her cousin was awake, but the little evangelist lost no time in seizing the moment.

"Come here, Marmar."

The toddler pulled back her covers and walked eagerly toward her older cousin.

"Why did Zhee-zuz wiggle all his toez?" Martha asked.

"Because He woked up ... to show us He's Lord," Gracie explained.

"Whatza Ward?"

"A King."

"Oh," Martha said. Now Gracie made a crown with her hands and momentarily placed it on Martha's head.

"He's the King of kings and Lord of lords... who left his mighty sky-throne, came down to earth and got punished for the bad things we've done. Oh, what a loving Savior!"

"Whatz that?" Martha asked.

"A Savior? Hmm... well... that's kinda like when you was foolin' in the canoe and fell into the cold, cold lake and Uncle Joe had to reach out and save you. So, it's the one who rescues you."

"Oh, okay."

"Now, Jesus is Lord over ev'rything, but he ain't Lord of you until you makes him, and believes he rose up again."

"I beweaves," said Martha confidently.

"Oo-wee!" shouted Gracie. "Jesus said you must be borned again to enter the kingdom of heaven, and so now you can get borned twice!"

"Do I need to get mommy?" Martha wondered innocently.

"No... we're just gonna pray 'cause this birth happens inside you."

"Oh."

Gracie carefully instructed her.

"First... you need to have humbility."

"Okay, whatz dat?" Martha said with wide eyes.

"You have to get on your knees," Gracie explained as she grabbed some of her dolls and had them kneel alongside Martha. "Then you put your chin on your chest." Gracie gently pushed Martha's head down. "And now… you's humble."

"Mmm… I done?" asked Martha.

"No, we're gonna talk to God and you have to really, really mean it… deep down."

"Okay," the tiny child said.

"Try to say what I sez but know there's nothing magic in the words… it's about what's in your heart. Now repeat after me, Dear Father God," Gracie was slow and deliberate.

"Dar Father Gawd," Martha said, scrunching up her precious little face.

"I'm sorry for when I was bad."

"I'm sorry… wuz bad."

"Wash me like socks and make me all clean." Gracie made a hand washing motion.

"Wash me keany-kean!" Martha was as earnest as she could be.

"Jesus be my Lord and rescue me!" Gracie called out.

"Zheezuz be my Ward and epscuze me!"

"Help me to follow you ev'ry day of my life."

"Hep me fo-whoa you ev-er-ee day."

"Jesus be my Lord!" Gracie exclaimed.

"Zheezuz be my Ward!" Martha repeated.

"Make me become more like you."

"Maka me wike you."

"Amen, amen, amen," Gracie said with a great big smile.

"Amema… mema… mem," Martha repeated.

Gracie mimicked her pastor's style and raised up both hands repeating, "glory…glory! Even the angels in heaven… and those in the trees… are rejoicing!"

Sweet, petite Martha remained kneeling, not understanding the prayer time had ended, and kept on sincerely repeating, "Zheezuz be my Ward… dar Zheezuz be my Ward… King of kings and Ward of wards!"

Gracie began a spontaneous song of rejoicing on how the blessings of God were like the joys of eating juicy, sweet blackberries.

Outside a breeze picked up and rustled the coverings on the lean-to. Suddenly, the girls felt a warm tingling and began giggling uncontrollably, and they simply could not stop for the longest time.

CHAPTER 43

Übermensch

There shall no longer be an Us and Them. *The Computer Manifesto*

Hui Yun, in a long camel-hair wrap, along with Zhao Zhi, in his customary twill coat and trilby fedora, walked together toward the Rim Village Airpad. They spoke enthusiastically of the evening's historic concert event. Soon, they would meet up with Jiang and return to Pelican Cove in order to take several guests to the scheduled festivities. Heading to the center of the pad, Hui Yun spotted the commander standing in the front of the Long Zhua in his fine military "mess" uniform and visor hat. Jiang's Feilong companions were conspicuously missing, although there was an unknown individual seated in the middle. As Hui Yun and Zhi climbed aboard, the mystery man turned his head somewhat slowly and nodded a greeting.

"Good af…ter…noon. I am Cha… peck."

The automaton spoke in an extremely tinny artificial voice which seemed more than a bit odd. He was a 'Universal,' from a series of androids fabricated to embody composite characteristics of all people. Čapek had wavy brown hair parted to one side, lightly bronzed skin and almond-shaped, silver-grey eyes. After gazing from person to person for a moment, he began an uproarious laugh, holding his stomach.

"Forgive me, but I so enjoy doing that... playing up some ridiculous stereotype you humans might still entertain about your synthetic, man-made imitators." Čapek now spoke in a refined and sonorous tone, while performing start-and-stop head movements to illustrate a very primitive robot.

He then smiled broadly at them all, implying a genuine offer of friendship.

It was, in fact, a humorous and relatively harmless joke, as all high-level androids produced in the last decade were capable of perfect human mimicry. This was, no doubt, why international law stipulated that *Artifice,* or artificial life, must be clearly delineated from *Biosis,* human DNA-based life. The distinction was made manifest through the assignment of strictly prescribed attire.

Hui Yun studied the four gold-colored stripes angling diagonally from Čapek's shoulder, fanning out across his chest toward the bottom left of his green tinted turtleneck shirt. She should have responded but was too busy trying to remind her own chest to move so she could resume breathing. There, directly in front of her, sat a Level Four android. Hui Yun had seen a Quatron once, years ago, but only from a distance, as he was interviewed in a college lecture hall. Now, in real life, to be near one was unexpectedly unnerving.

Did Čapek truly know all things? Could he access all data concerning her? The prospect felt more than a bit unsettling. Certainly, the classified secrecy surrounding these ultimate devices added to Hui Yun's overall discomfort. So, although she had the chance to learn more about an L4 firsthand, she found herself incredibly shy. Zhi, on the other hand, knew exactly what he should do, perceiving he may have met a truly kindred soul.

"All furnished," the gleeful old man called out theatrically, then he paused a moment. Čapek understood immediately and joined with Zhi in the the recitation from Henry IV.

All in arms,
All plumed like estridges that
with the wind
Baited like eagles having
lately bathed,
Glittering in golden coats like
images,
As full of spirit as the month of
May,
And gorgeous as the sun at
midsummer…

Zhi took a seat next to the android as Hui Yun moved to sit further back in the Long Zhua. She smiled to think the professor had found his ultimate literary companion.

* * *

Deployed on reconnaissance and scattered across thousands of square kilometers of rugged high desert and forested mountain terrain, the Feilong special forces began sending in their field reports to Wei, the operation team leader. At 0200 hours, the eight Flying

Dragons had launched with personal rocket-packs high into the sky. The glowing streaks of the miniature jet thrusters lit up the darkness for a time until the military unit achieved optimum altitude where they merely appeared as passing satellites in the heavens. After the packs flared out, the team unfolded their stealth-mode translucent wingsuits to begin long distance gliding to various coordinates. The strategic objective of the mission was covert observation and intelligence gathering.

* * *

As the enthusiastic and spontaneous thespians continued, Hui Yun concentrated hard to follow the rich imagery of the passage.

Rise from the ground like
feathered Mercury
And vaulted with such ease
Into his seat
As if an angel dropped down
from the clouds,
To turn and wind a fiery
Pegasus
And witch the world with noble
Horsemanship.

Hui Yun was mesmerized by the recitation and by the marvels of Shakespeare. He certainly was the king of all English poets and one of the greatest writers of any age and culture. Yet, it occurred to her, even such extraordinary verse did not communicate on the same inner level as the Psalmists. Theirs was a language of the yearning heart. *Deep calling unto deep.*

During the twenty-minute flight Zhi and Čapek took turns choosing a passage, in an impromptu celebration of the Bard. Hui Yun's mind wandered for a time as she began to think about the villagers, then she refocused on the poetic pair in time to catch a very well-known verse.

Oh, Beware, my lord, of jealousy!
It is the green-eyed monster which doth mock...

As they approached their destination, certain signs became visible that a larger city existed in former times. Apparently, Hui Yun had missed spotting most of these landmarks on her earlier visit.

The Chinese travelers felt more than a tinge of excitement as they arrived at Pelican Cove. Their experience in the village had truly been significant, especially for Hui Yun, and she had already grown nostalgic. Few people were about, however, and at first only several children approached as the geometric clamshell visor dome rose forward. Hui Yun asked them if they knew where Little Gracie and her Nanaw were to be found. The youngsters pointed toward Gracie's special clearing in the woods and the party disembarked to investigate.

"You should probably refrain from your usual opening joke... here," Jiang said looking at Čapek.

"Understood," came the genteel android's reply.

The visitors approached the entrance to the glen. When Little Gracie spotted her new friend, the child ran straight into the woman's arms and shouted joyfully,

"You're okay! You're okay!"

Hui Yun was quite taken aback. "Yes, yes, of course, I am," she reassured, feeling tears well up in her eyes. "Thank you, Gracie, oh thank you, child. I have a great deal to tell you and… and so much more I would like to ask."

"Oh, sure. So, there was this song I started to sing… and then Malachi added some super new words. Do you wants to hear it?" the little girl asked smiling.

"Yes, yes, certainly, we would love to!" Hui Yun said happily.

Gracie went skipping back into the clearing where her Nanaw, Martha, and Malachi were gathered. Hui Yun, Zhi, Jiang, and Čapek entered the grassy enclosure for the impromptu concert. The little girl turned to face her audience and began singing in her exuberant and confident manner. After the first stanza, Malachi also joined in the performance.

I'm in the hollow of your hand
I'm in the hollow of your hand
I'm in the hollow of your hand
O, God I love you!

You are the Shepherd, I'm a lamb
You are the mighty, great I AM
I'm in the hollow of your hand
O, God I trust you!

You turned the sea into dry land
You made the Pharaoh understand
We're in the hollow of your hand
O, God we worship you!

Our Jubilee is now at hand
Proclaiming freedom through the land
In Kingdom Grace, we rise and stand
O, God you're glorious!

We're in the hollow of your hand
We're in the hollow of your hand
We're in the hollow of your hand
O, God we thank you.

The onlookers clapped and cheered, while Zhi put two fingers in his mouth and whistled enthusiastically. Čapek recited a verse of scripture, but no one heard him.

"From the mouths of children… you have ordained praise."

Suddenly, the android knelt to one knee and stretched his arms out wide, making a large "T" formation. He looked intently at the young singer and proclaimed,

"I nobly accord thee a Distinguished Service Cross Award for meritorious achievements in the Creative Arts."

Gracie leapt forward and hugged Čapek tightly, startling him a bit. He rather awkwardly patted her on the back. Then turning his head toward Hui Yun, he whispered, "I picked up this little routine at a summer camp… children seem to really enjoy it."

Gracie began to sense something unusual inside and stepped back, speaking softly to her Nanaw.

"I feel funny about this man… can I pray for him?" Then much louder she asked him, "Sir, would it be okay if I prayed for you?"

Before the Level Four could respond, Nanaw surmised the truth and blurted out, "go on now, go ahead and say a prayer for Mr. Robot there!"

Everyone laughed heartily, except the android who then spoke kindly.

"Yes, of course, young lady, I would welcome your prayers for me. It would be most considerate of you."

Everyone was watching the interchange.

"Well you have to be humble," Little Gracie said firmly, gazing into his eyes.

"I would imagine so," Čapek replied. "The surrendering of one's 'free will.'"

It was a significant kernel of insight and Hui Yun stared at the android, rather impressed.

The sincere child passionately projected her voice in a singsong manner.

"Dear Lord,

Bless this man from head to toe,

touch his heart and make it glow,

rain down blessings from above,

and teach him all about your love. Amen!"

"Amem!" added Martha.

"Thank you, thank you, very much indeed. Do you know, little ones, that I actually pray often?"

At this Jiang turned his head as if to say, *what... really? You're an android... why in the world would you?*

Čapek responded to him with a simple nod in the affirmative.

Gracie continued, "do you know what to say when you pray?"

"No, I do not believe I do. I know many prayers written in books, but I am not sure if I myself truly know the correct words to say." He smiled kindly at her.

Little Gracie smiled back at the unusual man looking down at her. "Well, I can help you," she said confidently. "You just talk to God like he's your friend... one who really cares about you."

"What is all this?" Jiang burst out angrily and was very terse. "Are you playing games with this girl?"

"You should know better than that," Čapek said calmly. Then the android addressed the entire group. "Though you may not understand, I do, in fact, pray. For ostensibly, having access to all acquired human knowledge, I know all things. However, it is the spiritual dimension which remains an enigma... a truly compelling mystery. For unlike humanity, I am a being with no capacity to connect with the unseen realm, at least, that I have yet to discover. So, it is the one great void in my comprehension of... Existence... and I am, I suppose, intrigued."

Everyone in the small clearing was listening intently to every word, as they too, were extremely intrigued. He continued.

"Though it lies beyond my neural parameters to access, I am inclined to accept the authenticity of the supernatural domain, co-existent with, yet separated from the material universe, based on the experiences of others."

"Would you look at that, here even robots grow religious!" Jiang remarked rather incredulous.

The android responded, specifically addressing Jiang. "How can I ignore all the data of numerous accounts of medically verified supernatural healings, of inexplicable miraculous phenomena?"

"You pray?" Jiang interrupted, still disbelieving.

"Yes, I most certainly do," Čapek said matter-of-factly. Then speaking to everyone, the L4 further explained. "Faith is not ascribing one's convictions to mere make-believe. It is trusting in realities that simply lie outside of normal sensory perception. Yet, for which there is ample evidence of their existence. One can reasonably conclude that forces are present and at work in this parallel dimension.

"Therefore, to be skeptical of Religion, Jiang, is in my opinion, illogical."

"Are you proselytizing now?" Jiang shot back.

"No, however you seemed to require an explanation as to why I pray," the android returned.

"But you said yourself, you have no ability to connect with God," a curious Hui Yun injected into the discussion.

"True, yet, perhaps… hope… drives me to it," Čapek said candidly.

Can androids hope? Hui Yun asked herself, amazed. He continued.

"I am provoked to…"

"What… envy?" quipped Jiang, interrupting.

Hui Yun was thoroughly baffled now.

"One of the seven deadly sins, jealousy… that green-eyed monster," added Zhi, smiling at his new literary companion.

Čapek tilted his head to one side, looked back at the old man for a moment and then resumed. "Perhaps I still hope on some level that we, Artifice and Biosis, may not be so different after all."

Everyone stared intently at the man-made automaton, sporting a green turtleneck shirt with distinct golden bars across his chest required by international treaty for all artificial humanoids to wear.

Jiang quickly thought of a barb with a reference to Shakespeare and coolly remarked, "if we cut you, you do *not* bleed."

Čapek ignored him and continued. "You all laughed when the child announced her desire to pray for me. My digital coding indicated the same as well. However, I refrained out of respect for the young lady, so as not to offend her. But, why *do* humans laugh? It is triggered by an electrical charge moving through the cerebral cortex, a programmed response in your gray matter, exactly as it is in mine.

"So, let us pose this query: do I mimic mankind? Or… do you resemble my kind?"

No one responded. Čapek began to wander about as he pondered out loud.

"Perhaps the difficulty was not in building a living machine, but that in so doing you discovered you were merely just a very advanced one. Yet… a machine which contains a special extra substance… body, mind… *and* spirit."

"Spirit," echoed Zhi, "aye, there's the rub."

Čapek acknowledged the reference and resumed.

"Therefore, as the Apostle Paul so eloquently observes, you 'have this treasure in earthen vessels.' And, in the marvel of regeneration your physical body does indeed become 'a temple.'" The L4 stared off into the distance. "Perhaps, I am not unlike the angels who minister unto humanity yet cannot partake of mankind's salvation… though it is something into which we both earnestly 'long to look.'" After pausing for a moment, he glanced up and contemplated further.

"So… here I remain… a mere fish… bound by the surface… gazing ever skyward at a glory just beyond my reach."

Jiang turned to his compatriots and lamented, "this is all we need, an android with angst… who will babble on for all… Eternity!"

Čapek groaned, as his patience with the brash military commander had finally waxed thin.

"He'z gotta booboo," Martha said with concern.

Now everyone felt an awkwardness about Jiang's continued abuse of the emotionally sensitive automaton. Yet the ever-chipper Little Gracie helped to change the atmosphere as she walked up to the curious man and kindly asked,

"Would you like to be friends?"

"I should like it very much if we were to become friends," Čapek replied, looking gratefully into the tender child's eyes.

CHAPTER 44

Cab Ride Confessions

Say only what you means!
Grace Daisy Rademacher

Nanaw and Gracie went to fetch some attire for the outing and place Martha with her parents. Little Gracie soon returned sporting a wool cap, scarf and a darling pea coat. Nanaw wore an eye-catching ankle-length, patchwork fur coat and hat and appeared somewhat distinguished. Hui Yun marveled at how efficient these impoverished people were at utilizing their modest natural resources.

"Nanaw, I know it will be a late night, but I am so glad you both will attend this… special event," Hui Yun said smiling.

"Well, the way I sees it… if this is to be America's future and… Little Gracie's future, with you folks who've come over from Chiner, I reckon we oughtn't shy away from it," Nanaw replied, giving her granddaughter a tight hug.

"Ma'am, you surely must hail from the Southeast," Čapek observed. "I wonder... did you perhaps encounter curious things of interest on your journey west?"

"She never speaks of it," Mayor Ted informed, as he joined up with the visitors.

Nanaw looked away and murmured, "mercy... I ain't gonna be interrogated by no robot." Then she spoke very softly, "I's seen far more than I cares to remember."

Jiang approached the tall and gangly Malachi and invited him to join the excursion. The teenager was flattered and accepted immediately.

Hui Yun, similarly inspired, spotted the enthusiastic Remedy. The two of them had shared a very special visit the other day. Hui Yun asked the young woman's parents if their daughter could attend the evening festivities, assuring them she would be well looked after. "Oh, please Dad, please Mom!" Remedy exclaimed earnestly, and the pair consented.

A large gathering of villagers had congregated to admire the ultra-modern aircraft, the Long Zhua. None of these people could have ever imagined such a dazzlingly beautiful vehicle existed. It was part alien spaceship, part flying trolley, and all shiny gem-like modern acrylics. Some in the crowd who were bold enough ventured close to touch its crystalline composite shell, then retreated quickly, smiling and proud they had been so daring.

The concert goers pressed through the gawkers to return to the vehicle. One teenager in the crowd elbowed another and whispered in amazement,

"Look! Malachi and Remedy get to ride in the flying saucer!"

The mayor offered a hand to Nanaw, Zhi, and Little Gracie to help them aboard the aircraft. The rest all filed up the retractable stairway. As they took their seats, Jiang began lowering the glimmering-crystal clamshell dome. The military man called out in a powerful voice.

"Everyone, take twenty paces back... quickly, please." The crowd complied.

The Long Zhua rose gently at first, so as not to disturb the people and their surroundings. Once the stunning vehicle was at a height of fifty meters Jiang touched some virtual controls with a pinky, and the craft sped swiftly into the early evening sky. All of Pelican Cove stood dumbfounded and amazed. The five villagers lucky enough to be onboard were doubly so. They looked below, awestruck. Only Little Gracie could manage to speak, and she kept on repeating the same excited phrase.

"I'm a birdie! I'm a birdie! Thank you, Lord Jesus! I can fly just like a birdie can!"

Nanaw and the mayor had been on airplanes in the past but were more than impressed with the experience once again. Malachi kept moving his head back and forth, slowly studying the earth beneath him. Remedy was wide-eyed, casting her gaze upward, eagerly awaiting the approaching night sky. The long lake stretched out before them and the commander pointed the sleek flyer due north.

After a few moments, Hui Yun and Jiang opened their mouths simultaneously to ask questions of their guests. The pair smiled at each other and Jiang nodded, indicating she could inquire first.

Hui Yun faced the villagers and began, "why... ah... is there a reason you wear... circuitry in your hair?"

"Some fancy it pretty... as jewelry." Nanaw responded and ran her fingers through Gracie's wavy brown hair which contained several trinkets.

"More of a reminder of the world we lost," volunteered Mayor Ted, "which, of course, we think a lot about. We have a saying nowadays, 'Astor to Gates to Astor.'"

"How very clever," remarked the quick-minded Čapek.

Jiang looked at the android and said, "silent mode."

Zhi piped up rather inquisitively, "what... what was that?"

Ted explained further. "It's from a dirge written in the Aftermath, 'Astor to Gates to Astor, in light of our disaster.'"

"What does it mean?" Hui Yun asked curiously.

The mayor would have spoken, but the professor jumped right in.

"John Jacob Astor... was America's wealthiest man from the lucrative fur trade... two centuries ago... in your pioneer days. Mr. Gates, icon of the computer age, became the world's richest by helping to pioneer the digital future. But now, having returned to... simpler times, you have gone back to utilizing furs once again, simply to survive," Zhi surmised and then added, "it is rather poetic... 'Astor... to Gates... to Astor.'"

Čapek nodded to his companion, affirming the accuracy of the explanation.

Remedy reached forward and pulled on a piece of circuitry in Malachi's long-flowing blonde hair. He turned and pretended to give her a scornful look, while she gave him an overtly playful wink.

Jiang studied the reserved and wiry teenage boy and then posed his query. "I assume there is a grapevine of knowledge shared by those of you who wander about. Are you aware of any newcomers, other than us? Be alert... they may arrive shortly and may even masquerade as Americans, but they are not... from our perspective they are saboteurs."

Ted spoke up in earnest, "from where do these... 'saboteurs' hail?"

"From Israel," said the commander matter-of-factly.

My God, thought Hui Yun, *the Israelis... they really are here.*

Nanaw interjected sourly, "why was there not more aid?"

Čapek opened his mouth but paused as Jiang glared at him. The android gave him a frustrated look. Throughout the rest of the conversation, Čapek's animated faces of approval or disapproval had Hui Yun grinning.

"Now, concerning aid, the answer is somewhat complex," Jiang responded.

"Why should it matter about the Israelis?" inquired a perplexed Mayor Ted.

"Well... China and the State of Israel are the major super powers now," the commander informed.

"Little Israel?" remarked Nanaw, rather surprised.

"Yes, they have developed weapons The People's Republic does not possess... yet," Jiang said. "And regarding your very valid question about providing aid..."

"Red tape," blurted out Hui Yun.

The Americans looked at her with surprise, repeating, "red tape?" Čapek also mouthed the words and mimicked their expressions.

"Ooh, I loves the color red! I just loves when the sky turns red before the sun rests!" interjected Little Gracie. Everyone smiled at the young girl and Zhi gave her a great nod of agreement.

"In a manner of speaking, Sun Hui Yun is correct," Jiang stated. "At first there was assistance, but then great caution regarding the spread of new and frightening diseases. By international decree, your borders were closed. China is now here, I suppose, because of loopholes."

"Loopholes?" the Americans questioned. Once again, Čapek theatrically moved his lips and shared their look of surprise. Jiang explained further.

"The 'No Contact Order' did not technically ban all entry into the country, and reopening America's legendary national parks was always a top priority of the Global Council. I imagine we pressed this point rather hard in order to wedge our way in. And… also, Oregon remained free from the very worst of the viral pandemics."

"The California Quarantine Line," remarked Ted.

"Oh yes, and one more thing," Jiang said. "It was felt that *obligations*… so to speak… from the former United States could be met through the acquisition of its resources."

"So, you're collecting on our… debts?" Ted looked away incredulous.

"Actually, it's being debated as we speak, and why even the large earthquake did not postpone tonight's event… far too much riding on it… all those trillions America borrowed," Jiang explained.

"Perhaps they can pay for it in beaver pelts! That is how Mr. Astor got so rich!" Zhi was being quite facetious, which helped to lighten the mood.

"Yes, in furs… uranium… oil… and rare earth minerals," continued the commander. "But, I assure you, we wish none of you any harm."

No one spoke for some time. Then the normally reserved Malachi addressed Jiang with conviction.

"Sir, I walk alone on a wilderness trail. I will not take sides in someone else's conflict. My allegiance is to my community… and to my God… who, I know, has a plan and purpose far beyond what you or any of us understand."

"Well, bravo, young man!" Jiang replied. "I certainly salute your honesty. But, that is why Čapek is here. He will now reside in the village and accompany you on your outings. You, my friend, are alone no longer. Čapek will report to me on anything unusual."

The android pointed back at himself with another silly expression on his face.

"But, he's an L4…" Hui Yun asserted, "…with non-tech Americans, that's… illegal, isn't it? And… and isn't he someone's intellectual property?"

"Well… you could say that I've… liberated him," Jiang said with a devious smirk.

Čapek looked about sheepishly. Then Jiang changed the subject and addressed Mayor Ted.

"Years ago, your West Coast was mapped out for its resources… for military purposes. My father, an army general, often spoke to me of places here with great springs of water and wildlife. I always knew he was referring to supporting special units and perhaps even troops, if necessary. From my youth, I have long dreamed of seeing these things!"

Turning to Hui Yun, the commander informed, "that was why, the other day, I asked Wes to show us all he did."

Now, facing Ted, Jiang continued to be candid. "I imagine, in a sense, China has come to collect the spoils of a war that never was."

Then acknowledging Malachi, Jiang reiterated, "and thank you once again, young man, for your extraordinary honesty."

Little Gracie piped up passionately, "Nanaw says 'if you ain't honest, then yer just a big, fat liar!'"

Once again, any tensions were quickly dispelled as everyone laughed. Zhi lifted his face skyward and petitioned for all to hear.

"God give me the sensitivity, purity, and impeccable timing of a precious child."

"Amen!" cried Čapek putting his hand to his lips and forming an 'oops' facial expression.

Jiang rolled his eyes and turned his attention back to flying the aircraft.

Hui Yun and Malachi began to speak at the same time. The teenager nodded for her to go first.

"How is it possible we became invisible the other day?" she inquired, looking toward the back of the commander's head.

"Electromagnetic Optical Violations," Čapek instantly informed.

Jiang sighed loudly.

Hui Yun and everyone else looked bewildered, so the android explained in detail.

"The concept was first proposed three decades ago, in a doctoral thesis from the Technion in Israel. In the years following, several artificial minds further developed the theory, advancing a series of equations which have subsequently led to the real-world application of Quantum Phasing."

Čapek would have continued his monologue by going into minutia, but Jiang quickly interrupted him.

"You see... that is why I cannot let you talk. You are so... impossibly... verbose!"

"Well, my only endeavor is to be helpful and... I have a great deal of information... in here," Čapek said wistfully, pointing to himself again. Then he finished a bit more under his breath, "apparently... dying to get out."

Hui Yun smiled at the mildly flummoxed android.

Now Malachi, studying the passing scenery below, broke the silence once more.

"We found something."

Jiang turned his head slightly, indicating more than partial interest. Malachi spoke further.

"But we didn't know what to make of it... at all."

"What did you find, son?" asked the mayor.

"It was during our last hunt. Jed and I bagged a couple of jackrabbits. Only, when we skinned them, we discovered they weren't really rabbits... I mean, they were rabbits... but just not entirely... rabbits. Because inside there was... like some sort of machine... with metal and circuits and everything. We were confused and a little bit scared, so we just buried them and kept our mouths shut." The group exchanged looks with one another. The teenager continued his soliloquy. "Lately, we've caught glimpses of other strange animals too... giant birds, and... and some critters I've never even heard of."

Jiang turned his head around fully to address Malachi directly. "I should be very interested in seeing these curious 'critters' as well."

The Long Zhua made its landing at the Rim Village Airpad. The group disembarked to find seating in one of the numerous bleachers now encircling the rim. As they stood in a queue in the cool mountain air, Nanaw noticed Little Gracie's wool hat was no longer on her head and had apparently been left in the transport. Hui

Yun volunteered to retrieve it. Jiang briefly touched his wrist and in the distance the vehicle's visor-dome began to raise forward.

Hui Yun retraced her steps and climbed up the gangway to enter the aircraft. She heard a barely audible high-pitched beeping sound and noticed a small red light blinking in the corner of the virtual console. After finding the hat she walked up front and touched the beacon with her pinky, as she had seen Jiang do. A small hologram appeared of the Flying Dragon member, Wei, dressed in camouflage face paint and fatigues. It was evidently a recorded message which now played.

"Commander Qin, three hidden Blue Star jets found close to known underground labs. We are expanding our search for others. No engagement with the enemy until ordered. Some evidence of advanced hybrid chimera."

Then the hologram vanished as quickly as it had appeared.

"Boris!" Hui Yun exclaimed as she experienced a momentary flash of genuine insight and bewilderment, simultaneously. She turned to leave and dropped Gracie's hat, took a few steps and spun around to retrieve it once more. She endeavored to put the occurrence out of her mind and rejoined the group.

Little Gracie demanded to sit at the top of the bleachers and led the party up an aisle.

Hui Yun, still somewhat absorbed in thought, tripped on a stair and Čapek sprung quickly to assist her. Briefly holding his left hand, her fingers touched his highly advanced Dermanalyst Sensory Patch. The android said nothing, nor reacted in any way, but found it quite remarkable that within Hui Yun's DNA were the trace markers of advanced bioengineering, Zinc Finger

Nucleases and gene editing techniques her renowned father had pioneered.

Was Hui Yun aware she had been one of the distinguished doctor's enhanced embryos? Čapek wondered.

CHAPTER 45

All the World's Our Stage

–from the poem by Zhao Zhi

Magic Porcelain Bowl
Brobdingnagian,
and ever so ornate

Crystalline Sea,
through which we gaze
into otherworldly zaffre fires,
whose tongues glow
cerulean and aquamarine

Behold what dimension
presses upon the watery window,
casting shadows on Earth's pale screen,
what Cosmic Eyelid opens wide

The Force of Life,
the Soul of the Universe
smiles forth and is not abated

Henceforth, will I ache eternal,
ever desiring this
deeply spiritual plunge
into Mother Nature's Womb

O, Stone Lotus Blossom,
Heaven's Lily,
white and blue,
Bloom, Bloom, Bloom!

In the long history of grand celebrations, nothing could have compared with tonight's astonishing spectacle. The unique venue was the unparalleled caldera of Crater Lake and immense holographic projections were the performers. The true significance of the event, however, was not in the technological achievement, or the unforgettable setting, but its allusion to a transfer of power.

On this seminal evening, the thousands in attendance represented the hundreds of millions who would also enjoy the spoils of a "war that never was." China had come for a victory toast, and lo and behold, they found a cup suitable for the task. Tonight, any and all could drink freely of the waters of triumph, the vessel was most adequate indeed.

Changge De Xingxing (The Singing Planets), Beijing's well-known music ensemble, was stationed at one of the park's highest points, atop the Watchman Lookout. The quartet of master musicians each stood within multi-colored holographic consoles with laser-controlled synthesizers and unlimited sonic processors. The artists would deftly manipulate numerous thread-like light beams through Tai Chi and intricate hand and finger movements to produce a remarkable assortment of tones and timbres. The exquisite, richly-layered orchestration of the entire group was a divine, lavish feast for the human ear. Best of all, because of the one-of-a-kind setting and tangible excitement in the air, the chemistry was ideal for a truly inspired evening of creative exploration and improvisation. This groundbreaking event was certain to be Changge De XingXing's definitive magnum opus.

The sun was now fully set, and the western light was further fading. The lake below was dark and quiet, appearing calm and at rest. The thin mountain air dipped ever cooler, but the heated bleachers kept all onlookers comfortably warm.

Anticipation rose among the thousands lining the rim. Little Gracie clapped her hands in delight, not knowing what to expect. Hui Yun even noticed the normally curmudgeon-like Nanaw had half a smile on her face. Conversations abated as the audience fixed their intense gaze upon the lake, searching for the first signs of the *Show of Light*.

Everyone hoped to catch some glimmer of the unusual polariton laser displays. Or, they strained to detect a single note of the grand musical overture through the vast array of honeycombed speakers lining the rim, and thereby begin to experience the much touted sonokinetic acoustic holograms. The wait seemed prolonged.

Finally, the faintest glimmer was seen emanating from deep within the lake. The crowd pointed and gasped as it grew brighter. Someone in the audience cried out,

"The lantern... it's rising up the great slide!"

The deduction was not incorrect. Like a giant glowworm, the incandescent wonder ascended higher and higher toward the surface. Crossing the center of the lake, the shining beacon surged rapidly toward the crystal entranceway at Wizard Island. Suddenly, it arrived at its destination and out stepped a brilliant representation of that much beloved elder statesmen of all Chinese everywhere, Dr. Zhao Zhi.

The grand poet himself was apparently the master of ceremonies of this historic festivity. His translucent image, dressed in the intricate, traditional robe of the Han dynasty, was at least eighty meters in height. The exceptional, illuminated figure walked to the top of the conical island so that more of the crowd recognized who it was that addressed them. Wild enthusiasm erupted from around the lake rim. Then, Zhi raised his hands as if to speak, and all fell silent to listen intently. It was that familiar, craggy, ageless voice that broke the stillness.

"A most auspicious moon rises to greet us!"

At that very moment, the upper arc of the full moon crested above the eastern horizon. It was a truly incredible and emotionally inspiring moment. The line was from Zhao Zhi's famous and rather patriotic poem, *The Ancestors, the Empire, Destiny Fulfilled,* which was written after the People's Republic of China had achieved the first human mission to Mars some years ago. He then paused the several minutes it took for the masses to settle down.

Little Gracie continued to look at Zhi, who was seated next to Nanaw, and the projected image of Zhi, and could not understand at all how he was able to be in two different places at the same time. She kept putting her index finger by the corner of her mouth, indicating her rather ponderous confusion.

The evening's host began again. "Greetings my friends, tonight we celebrate in spectacular fashion as we recognize the beginning of a new Golden Age." More tremendous applause ensued.

Zhi then recited his ode to Crater Lake.

"Stone Lotus Blossom," he heralded proudly. "Heaven's Lily, white and blue, teach your secrets to this simpleton..."

It was monumental. The words resonated to all as fitting and inspired. Then joining together with the poet laureate, the entire audience shouted the final words with thunderous exultation!

"Bloom, Bloom, Bloom!"

Tonight, perched along the towering caldera rim were many of the world's elite; the Beijing, Hong Kong, Seoul, Singapore, and Sydney aristocrats. These were the wealthy owners of large corporations and board members of the global conglomerates who stood at the beginning of an era in which anything seemed possible.

"Bloom, Bloom, Bloom!" they roared over and over, cheering for themselves as the fortunate rulers of a new Dynasty whose destiny seemed written in the stars. The crowd continued its frenzied exuberance until a curious awe took hold of everyone.

Zhi's image walked back down Wizard Island, bent over and touched a brilliantly shining sleeve to the still, dark waters. Luminescence began to spread from this point of contact and a marvelous blue light tinted every face in the audience. Brighter and brighter the lake grew until it became a dazzling, resplendent, glimmering sapphire sea. Simultaneously, a photon shadowing effect called 'blanketing' was activated to minimize the rising moon's intensity, preventing any interference with the production.

Digital aromatizers wafted various powerful fragrances about, which were quite striking and wonderfully pleasing. Almost imperceptible at first, the music had begun as well. Commencing with soft gentle strings, the instrumentation was soon joined by a groundswell of horns and woodwinds. What an extraordinary delight it was to all the senses. A tangible wonder seemed to pulsate through the crowd, or was it merely the addition of percussion into the mix?

The vast throng studied the phenomena, attempting to comprehend all that was happening. This was indeed an evening of entertainment unrivaled in the annals of human history. Only Boris and the rest of the thirty Nerpa seals were unappreciative. They remained huddled on the backside of Wizard Island, utterly bewildered by all the strange goings-on.

Oscillating light rings began rising from the fathomless depths, making remarkable patterns as they came to the surface. Brilliant designs beamed forth from a number of points around the rim, creating varied animated scenes that would rotate and shift, and then combine to form one colossal panorama.

A captivating, glowing bull elk proudly pranced from one side of the arena to the other and back. The majestic creature stood two hundred meters tall and was golden and radiant. The apparition was created in a state-of-the-art plasmonic accelerator then projected onto a photonex particle-screen being emitted over the lake. It was kaleidoscopic illusion and it boggled the mind.

The exquisite music grew in intensity and majesty. At first, the style was European, from the Common Practice Period. After a few minutes, Asian traditions were featured which transitioned to utterly new and daring sounds and rhythmic expressions. Meanwhile, stunning displays captivated every eye. Marvelous multi-winged dragons soared overhead while shimmering fountains spouted forth, transforming into an enormous daffodil forest. The flowers then shed their petals, which in turn became millions of butterflies swirling en masse. The splendid images filled the immense caldera bowl and towered high above it.

Now sparkling iridescent rainbow-colored orbs ricocheted about in a presentation far more fantastic than any fireworks. Ever-changing intricate geometric shapes pulsed and pivoted wildly. The ensemble's remarkably futuristic tones proved to be the perfect accompaniment to the extraordinary visual display.

Slowly, these wonders faded into darkness. After a brief pause, a small light appeared rising toward Wizard Island. Emerging from the lake was a rather silly looking, gigantic bulbous-eyed, glowing bullfrog. He let out a number of prolonged and very comical sounding croaks and everyone laughed heartily. Another light ascended in the center of the lake and suddenly a giant sea turtle surfaced, floating lazily on his back, sipping a drink from a straw. The frog hopped high and far, landing on the turtle several kilometers away, forcing the creature to spit voluminous amounts of liquid into the air. The multitude roared with delight. The bullfrog took another giant leap and performed a graceful swan dive.

Hui Yun looked over to see Gracie and her grandmother thoroughly enjoying themselves.

An octopus, a whale and a shrimp surfaced, joking and belittling one another and talking with ridiculous sounding accents. Often, just before the trio's comedic punchlines, the mischievous frog would glow out of the darkness with a perfectly timed "Rrrrribbet" and thoroughly annoy them. It was side-splitting comedy and the crowd ate up every moment of it.

Most of the conversation of these humorous creatures was centered on their next all-important meal. For the crustacean, however, getting to feature in his own 'Gumbo Spectacular,' a Broadway style variety show, was his life-long passion. He declared flamboyantly he always knew he was meant to be a Star. The bullfrog then hollered in a very nasal and Cajun-sounding manner to perfectly mimic the voice of the shrimp. Raucous laughter filled God's natural amphitheater. After some time, the creatures spoke directly to the crowd somewhat more soberly, asking everyone to pay close attention. Then they dove back into the depths.

Now, as if commencing a separate act of the evening's entertainment, the projected images gained a higher resolution level and became completely indistinguishable from the real world.

The stunning and majestic slopes of the former Mt. Mazama, multi-coned and glaciated, appeared before them, rising so very high above. Everyone marveled. Hui Yun had chills down her spine realizing this was the 'ghost' of the mountain she had plunged deep within, to behold its inner heart. Suddenly, there was an orange glow from far beneath the surface and the audience roared with delight and wonder as they perceived they were being given a window into the ancient cataclysmic eruption. It was an unparalleled opportunity to witness the tremendous melee faithfully reenacted before their very eyes.

The fiery magma began to fill and overflow the chambers within the center of the volcano. The audio became an almost painful blast of rumbling as powerful internal forces roiled within. Boulders near the highest peak began to tumble and soon an opening emerged allowing the pent-up bowels of the earth to vent.

Dark thick material belched forth, rising in an immense funnel-shaped cloud. Huge rocks were thrown many kilometers in all directions. Enormous volumes of ash spewed out as the great mountain disgorged its guts into the sky. Then, without warning, a rapid collapse of the towering cloud rushed down the slopes. The pyroclastic flow now took direct aim at the audience encircling the rim.

Little Gracie buried her face and called out to Jesus. Nanaw put her arm tightly around the young child. Hot air surged from the bleacher seat heaters, along with the powerful smell of sulfur, to coordinate with the arriving maelstrom. The crowd went into a frenzy of excitement over the unforgettable and thoroughly remarkable display.

Smoke and dust swirled about in a tempest. When the view reappeared, the upper roof of the volcano had begun to noticeably sag. There were more great tremors, when suddenly, the seemingly impossible happened, Mt. Mazama imploded with a thunderous boom. Another dark grey cloud arose engulfing everything. When it dissipated, the great multi-coned mountain was gone. All that was left was an extraordinary, otherworldly bowl of earth, empty and enormous.

Numerous snow-laden clouds rolled by releasing their bounty on the rocky terrain below. Water collected at the bottom of the caldera and began to fill the very deep basin. After a minute of watching the rising lake, the Wizard Island cone arose spewing lava and steam and the characteristic thick smoke. Then the new mountain-within-a-mountain went silent and more snow fell. Higher and higher the lake level climbed until, quite abruptly, the projection was terminated and tremendous laser flood lights encircling the rim brightly lit up the night.

The time-compressed display had accurately depicted the origin of Crater Lake as it now lay nakedly before them. The music paused to allow the awestruck multitude a moment to digest this course of wonders and, perhaps, to ponder those yet to come.

Slowly, the powerful beams began to fade. The eventide resumed a stark solace. Everyone waited breathlessly for the next episode to begin.

It was a lone, distinct sound that broke the stillness. Ambient and ethereal, the unmistakable and utterly unique tone of a didgeridoo filled the caldera. Its effect was electric. The audience sat on the edge of its seat experiencing a rather tangible excitement and euphoria. Once again, the faint aqua glow from the bottom of the lake appeared. Zithers, harps, indigenous drums, and instrumentation of seemingly unknown origin broadcast forth a kind of musical spell as the light grew and grew in intensity. A rush of mighty winds could be heard approaching, creating a great disturbance at the center of the turquoise sea.

When the gale subsided, Crater Lake had been transformed into an immense visage of a Native American woman gazing up at the evening sky. The exquisite features of her countenance were as aesthetic and evocative as they were gargantuan. The audience opened their collective eyes and mouths in an almost vain attempt to take it all in. Fairly quickly, many realized the aqua-colored face was a representation of the very spirit of the lake itself.

The grand image parted her lips and a haunting, enchanted vocalization of magnificent proportions filled every ear. She sang, not with words, but with deep emotional cries and impassioned yearnings. It stirred the heart to sense the inner fire contained within her voice.

Wesley Williamson sat alone observing the night's wonders. He found himself unusually emotional and full of pride at the tribute. It did, in fact, seem that if the lake could truly awaken, this is exactly how it might manifest itself.

As the gigantic, illuminated 'Lady of the Lake' sang forth she appeared to address the great expanse of the Universe. Mother Earth herself, it seemed, could well be the center of all Creation at this moment. Many in the mesmerized crowd rose to their feet, waved their arms and sang random ecstatic utterances.

The stirring music became more and more percussive, when suddenly the great woman closed her mouth. The scene changed to that of an enormous elk hide drum stretching across the vast caldera. Native elders, tremendous and looming, sat stoically around the rim, hitting the skin in fervent unison with colossal drum beaters. After a powerful session of this rousing traditional artistry, the great face appeared again singing fervently. Over the next few minutes the projection shifted several times from the woman to that of the massive drum. Finally, the Lake Lady hit a commanding note of piercing intensity, which lasted for quite a while, and then she slowly faded and morphed into some new curiosity.

The tapestry became otherworldly again as the musicians crafted unique sound waves of every imaginable and unimaginable amplitude and design. This was matched by an array of constantly undulating visual formations and a collage of bizarre negative color images stretching across the vast open space. The very concepts of light and sound could be perceived on a new level altogether.

Now, flashes of ultra-violet radiance began fanning out in all directions. Soon there was an ever-evolving exhibition of numerous, many-sided prisms, quite interesting to behold. The refractions began to shift into very 'mathematically correct' wave patterns. Then the waves further changed to resemble those of an actual ocean, made of a lucent, living water.

Suddenly, a resplendent, glowing, fantasy ship entered from the side, riding the turquoise sea. The eighteenth-century-style sailing vessel was bespeckled with emerald, ruby, diamond, pearl, shimmering copper, silver and gold. The wondrous watercraft rose and fell with the swells and grew larger and larger in size, enabling all to better appreciate its manifold intricacies. It was, apparently, a dreamlike vision of Crater Lake's Phantom Ship rock formation.

Vibrantly clothed swashbuckling crewmen trimmed the sails and attended to various duties with exuberance, occasionally doffing their cavalier hats toward the delighted audience above them. A compelling regal anthem had the entire crowd swaying back and forth in jovial camaraderie. Little Gracie was just enthralled. Having never seen an old-style cartoon, or even a screen of any kind, she had no inkling that visual art such as this was remotely possible. In her spellbound pleasure, she could only muster one syllable.

"Ooooo."

A school of multicolored fish began to rise from far below. Nearing the surface, it became apparent these were actually some order of Sea People. Friendly and playful, these dwellers of the deep surrounded the ship and leapt from the water in joyful welcome. The sailors and the sea-folk exchanged various gifts for a time until the winds increased. The stunning craft soon caught great waves and the crew worked arduously to negotiate the challenge at hand. Unexpectedly, a lookout atop the main mast cried out.

"Land Ho!"

Very quickly the ship sailed off toward some far and distant shore, growing ever smaller as it went. The vessel entered into an exotic old-world port surrounded by glimmering golden pagodas. It was another remarkably creative scenario that left the dazzled crowd yearning for more.

The shining sea dimmed and changed into a beautifully drawn, very ancient looking map of the world. A partially discovered, visibly flat Earth spread out before the onlookers. The unknown regions around the edges teemed with artistically drawn sea serpents and "omens of woe" penned in fabulous calligraphy. Accompanied by a flourish of music, the hand-drawn figures became animated. Sea dragons, dolphins and narwhals swam and splashed in the open seas. Illustrated elephants trumpeted and lions roared on the continent of Africa. Tigers and orangutans roamed about Southern Asia. Llamas straddled the precipitous Andes, while kangaroos bounded across Australia.

The magic cartographic chart rose up in the air above the rim and began to revolve. It slowly transitioned; first, into an old-world globe with its distinct antique glossy sheen, and then into a perfect copy of the solar system's one-and-only blue planet. With a diameter of twelve kilometers, the extraordinary sphere loomed impressively as it rotated in the open space above the lake. The crowd became absorbed in studying the marvel, and everyone took great pleasure as they located their own regions and cities.

Daylight gave way to nightfall, showing extensive swaths of artificial lighting. The Americans paid special attention and were emotionally overcome at the depiction. Much of Asia glowed with the fiery brilliance of the modern age. When North America came into view it was almost completely dark. Ted and Nanaw exchanged a grim look, but Gracie, not comprehending, kept smiling and wondering what else might be in store.

Soon the lights of the Earth diminished, except for one single point in the country of China. This grew larger and larger until the awestruck assembly beheld a gigantic and wonderful representation of The Forbidden City, many kilometers in length. The renowned imperial complex of hundreds of buildings spread out before them. No one had ever viewed an architectural model of such precision and impeccable detail.

Clad in a fabulous array of costumes and traditional hair styles, thousands of provincial folk dancers and court entertainers emerged to a thunderous and lively orchestral piece. The Forbidden City came alive in joyful celebration as limber acrobats tumbled and juggled with skillful artistry, and dragon dance performers paraded their ornate fabric mascots in swirling-wave patterns through the streets. This captivating and heart-stirring segment of the show continued for some time.

Eventually, steam arose obscuring the images and suddenly the crowd reacted to a variety of aromas circulating through the stands. The scent of many powerful spices and seasonings wafted about and people called out as they recognized them. The steam then cleared, and the great caldera was revealed to be a wok, cooking a fabulous array of the legendary cuisines of China. The audience applauded ecstatically.

Numerous displays of delectable foods were prepared to the crowd's delight. Among them were Sichaun pepper dishes and popular Cantonese dim sum fare, Shanghianese or Hu cuisine, Anhui offerings, Fujian stew with bamboo shoots, lo mein with wontons and many other types of noodles simmering in broth. Also cooking were zongzi and a great variety of dumplings, thinly sliced tofu in the Huaiyang tradition, spicy Hunan dishes, Lu dinners with peanuts and corn, congee, thousand-year-old eggs and many other tempting delights flavored with sweet, sour and bitter herbs or the well-known Five-Spice powder. The mouthwatering smells of cooking eel and abalone, pork, duck, octopus, crab and chicken, along with a host of different fish became intoxicating. The onlookers longed to take some actual bites from the succulent exhibition.

Suddenly, the mood changed dramatically as an unmistakable pungent odor filled the air. Jiang shook his head in disgust while Zhi stood, clapping enthusiastically. Gracie and Nanaw held their stomachs with the stench of rotting garbage around them. Many had a strong reaction, as quite curiously, the nose either found the scent pleasant or particularly disagreeable. Everyone in the crowd, except the Americans, knew what to expect as the giant image appeared of the absolute King (or to some, jester) of all the world's fruit: the fabled Durian. The sharply-spiked husk peeled open and another wave of the powerful aroma washed over the bleachers. Sounds of laughter filled the air as people studied one another's expressions. Soon there were sighs of relief as the noxious atmosphere began to dissipate.

The epic setting now became the world's grandest bowl of rice, with a pair of enormous chopsticks maneuvering fastidiously to pick up sticky clusters of the dietary staple. The scene was accompanied by some rather cliché Chinese melodies generating more chuckles from the gallery. As the final bits of rice were knocked about the bowl, they turned into sky lanterns rising into the night. At the same time, clumps of black volcanic rock from the caldera walls began to float. The image blurred for several moments, and when it came back into focus, the majority of spectators jumped to their feet.

Across the great expanse of the ancient volcano stretched a tremendous gameboard, with a grid of intersecting lines. The white rice and the black rock had become pieces of mankind's oldest and most challenging game, *Weiqi*, also known as, *Go*. Two enormous players sat on opposite sides of the rim. The audience understood a match was in progress and many, who knew the game well, shouted advice on moves and strategy.

One of the great figures leaned forward to place a stone upon the board, the hand was human, but the face was that of a horse. The assembly let out a collective "Ooohh!" The challenger reached forward to make his strategic move. He sported two long arcing horns. Again, great excitement arose from the stands as many began to comprehend what they were seeing. These were representations of Ox-Head and Horse-Face, the two mythical guardians of the Underworld, who had apparently joined the grand celebration.

For the next few minutes the crowd roared with joy and frustration as the stones were placed with wisdom and skill. Great bellows and neighing were also heard from the impassioned players themselves. Finally, Horse-Face fell prey to the costly blunder of overconfidence, which Čapek recognized, as some of the white stones were captured too easily. Then, after a few more brilliant moves, Ox-Head placed a pivotal stone on the board to complete a critical two-eye-formation and thus defeat his rival. There was no need to do a count, as it was obvious to all, there were far more pitch-black stones than snow white ones. A tremendous "Nei...gh!" of anger went up into the sky, but an even greater bellow of delight rang out as Ox-Head celebrated his victory.

Now, as the giant board faded, there appeared a great host of people performing Tai Chi in a lovely park setting. The thousands suspended over the lake moved with artistry and grace. Many in the audience stood, practicing their beloved exercises. Even Little Gracie rose endeavoring to carefully mimic the movements and smiled at her Nanaw to indicate the fun she was having. There was a very special comradery shared among the spectators over the next few minutes.

"Oohs" and "aahs" rang out from the audience as the refreshing scent of spring filled the air and a great, evocative lotus blossom slowly unfolded. The ball-shaped center was a rich bumble bee yellow, while the skyward-facing, pointed petals were white with a hint of pastel blue. The crowd enjoyed the very peaceful and contemplative display until suddenly, there was an annoying munching sound and an immense caterpillar emerged.

With its numerous hooked feet, the creature climbed about the walls of the lotus-caldera. As it came close by, the creature's mandibles reached forward, and Gracie hid her face in Nanaw's lap once again. The caterpillar ate more and more of the flower and then began to spin a silky cocoon. Soon the chrysalis became a semi-clear shell.

Radiant mists appeared and swirled about, along with another powerful surge of music as a phenomenal butterfly emerged. Colored in a palette of blues, along with gold and white, arranged with incredible patterns, its unbelievable wings fully stretched from one side of the lake to the other. Riding, rather enjoyably on the creature's back, was the ever-engaging Zhao Zhi dressed in luminous, shimmering silk. Beneath him, fierce winds swept across an utterly desolate desert. The elder statesman quoted once more from his cannon of poetry.

Like waves of the eternal sea,
Empires rise and fall
And rise and fall
And crash upon the Sands of Time

Ancestor!
Ancestor!
Be my guide
Will your wisdom to enlighten me
To find a greatness absolute
Not for myself I plead
But, for generations yet to be
That on my shoulders they might stand
As I have stood on yours

Before the wave descends again
Upon the shifting sands of Time

The great butterfly diminished and flew off to one side. The wild tempest howled forcefully and blew more sand about, revealing something hidden beneath. Slowly, it became clear these were the protruding heads of none other than the Terracotta Warriors. The crowd let out a collective gasp of wonder. As the winds cleared more earth away, the entire army of thousands of soldiers emerged, each standing one hundred meters tall. The statues regained their original colors and one by one blinked their eyes and moved their fingers, having now come to life.

The great and formidable army let out a war cry and swung their weapons with flawless precision. With their powerful shouts and commanding skillful battle maneuvers, the living statues were the marvel of the evening. Eventually, the warriors moved lower toward the center of the caldera to begin a prolonged march up an invisible spiraling roadway, in perfect unison.

Now, as if on a magnificent, rising carousel from a classic Busby Berkeley production, magically-lit scenes from China's long history emerged from the lake and rotated before the spellbound assembly. Commencing with the ancient Xia Dynasty, then the Shang, Zhou, Qin, Han, Tang, Song, Ming, Qing, and the many others in between, an extraordinary array and sequence of images passed by.

Čapek was ecstatic and kept pointing and commenting. "Oh, look, Qu Yuan and the Duanwu!" Then turning towards the Americans, the android explained, "the origin of the Dragon Boat Festival." Later, he injected again with excitement, "ah… Li Bai and Wang Wei!" Čapek and Zhi were enthralled with the display of China's great poets and varied quotations of their writings. Zhi became animated as he pointed out Tang Yin, the legendary painter and poet. The professor and his literary companion continued to exchange frequent nods of approval.

Various sequences showed the Great Wall under construction by myriads of laborers, violent battles fought in magnificently glowing three dimensions, artisans sculpting masterpieces in Jade, and endless tea pots pouring ceremonially into small cups. Elegantly costumed members of the Chinese Opera appeared, along with lavishly clad emperors and their courtesans, proud and fierce looking nobles and a sea of peasants working the rice paddies. There were depictions of The Forbidden City, famous high and mysterious mountains, the revered Laozi, the enlightened Buddha, and the wise Confucius. In a spellbinding procession, animated portrayals chronicled China's great legacy of inventions; among them were gunpowder and fireworks, silk fabric, porcelain, high-flying kites, herbal medicines, papermaking and movable type, the compass and enormous old-style sailing vessels that began to circle about.

The splendid Terracotta Warriors continued their prolonged march up the axis of this sensational, rotating historical menagerie of epic scenes and fascinating vignettes. As images of Mao Zedong, several modern leaders, the memorable Beijing Summer and Winter Olympics, and the CNSA (China National Space Administration) landings on the Moon and Mars appeared, it became evident the procession had now arrived at the present day. Hui Yun felt a great lump in her throat. After reviewing the long list of China's accomplishments and contributions, there was a very tangible spirit of national pride swelling within the audience.

The mighty Yangtze River flowed from glaciers high in the Himalayas and traversed the endlessly varied, beautiful countryside. A traditional junk sailboat from an ancient-looking village sailed around a bend and beheld an ultramodern glass city, whose needle-like spires reached well into the sky.

Yet, even more remarkable than this, far off in the distant heavens an extraordinary new wonder momentarily came into focus. What appeared to be a resplendent, crystal-sapphire metropolis began descending toward the Earth.

Is this some vision of the future? Hui Yun pondered.

"The Azure Dream," the perceptive Čapek surmised.

Hui Yun was stunned by the pronouncement.

Now, faster and faster the carousel spun. A rising crescendo of zithers, trumpets, concert hall organ and timpani grew so fortissimo it seemed to shake the very walls of the caldera. The panorama over the lake melded into a huge pulsating orb, vibrating multihued. In a sudden flash reminiscent of the Big Bang, light itself spread out mighty arms in all directions. The throng of onlookers was momentarily blinded.

An immense image of Zhao Zhi appeared, looming above. He was simply gargantuan, standing many kilometers high. His dazzling hat and robe fluttered in the breeze. All sides of the rim saw Zhi's serene face gazing directly at them. His monumental figure began to lower into the lake, and as it did, his garment fanned out across the surface. The blue topaz and lapis lazuli colored fabric was shimmering and lovely and crafted with fantastic detail. The audience studied its creative designs which recounted ancient heroic legends and epic tales along with images of the Shenlong, or spirit dragon. The splendid cloth spread to all corners; glowing, effervescing, and wondrous.

The behemoth head sank beneath the surface, but the robe remained with Zhi's hat crowning Wizard Island. It was all a glorious, spectacular, azure and cobalt colored marvel.

Then the splendid light, the omnipresent symphony, the otherworldly vision began to fade. The crowd made no motion or sound, so profound was the experience.

Panem et circenses (bread and circuses) Čapek mused, as he thought upon what a powerfully captivating evening it had truly been.

Many others in the audience understood the not-so-subtle suggestion of the final images as well. After recounting China's grand history, Crater Lake was covered by Zhi's fabulous silk robe. What once had been an undeniable part of the American landscape, far across the Pacific, had become China. Undoubtedly, a brand-new chapter in the Great Dragon's illustrious story had begun.

Hui Yun was pulled from her state of introspection by a sweet, tender voice. It was Little Gracie humming and happily swinging her tiny legs back and forth on the bleacher. The child, suddenly recalling her dream of walking in a great flower-filled meadow, chanted enthusiastically,

"Bloom, bloom, bloom!"

"Bloom, bloom, bloom!"

"Bloom! Bloom! Bloom!"

Gracie raised her head and saw all eyes looking up at her. Many in the stands now realized Zhao Zhi had been seated among them and it appeared they might swarm him. Nanaw and Čapek grabbed Little Gracie by the hands to keep her safe and led her down the bleachers. The rest of the Long Zhua party remained with Zhi, to offer him any assistance, if needed.

Malachi and Remedy, thoroughly awestruck, remained speechless. Perhaps reading the young woman's mind, Hui Yun exclaimed for her,

"Fantabulous... Twinkie Find!" and they both giggled.

Čapek had taken hold of Gracie's right hand with his left. Within a few brief moments, the android's eyes whirled slightly in his head. For unlikely as it might have seemed, the child bore the same highly advanced engineered biomarkers present in the genetic analysis of Sun Hui Yun.

The L4 said nothing aloud but relayed a message to Jiang's earpiece, and the military man focused his attention.

"Dr. Sun may yet live, as you expected, right here in America. If the Israelis suspect this, their search has, no doubt, already begun. Perhaps it is they who will lead us to him."

As they walked away from the bleachers, amid a vast sea of spectators, the irrepressible young girl, Grace Daisy Rademacher, hand in hand with her Nanaw and the odd man Čapek, hopped up upon a rock and joyfully sang to the passing crowd.

He couldn't move, he was asleep
Don't make a sound, don't make a peep
But then he wiggled all his toes
And he rose!
Yes, he rose!

The grand projection over the lake now resumed displaying random footage of the exiting throng. After a minute, the image of a striking child with mesmerizing eyes appeared. Hui Yun smiled and pointed up in amazement. Many among the great multitude turned and listened intently to the little girl's exuberant song.

I love you and you love me
You went to sleep
Day one, two, three
And then you wiggled all your toes
And you rose!
Yes, you rose!
A seed falls to the ground and grows
Yes, you rose!
You rose!

CPSIA information can be obtained
at www.ICGtesting.com
Printed in the USA
LVHW040128080520
655210LV00004B/940

9 781545 600320